"We can be friends..."

"Friends?" Lorenzo almost laughed at that, his eyebrows shooting up in an expression of contempt that made her burn. "I'm sure you'd like nothing better, Isobel."

"What does that mean?"

"Oh, only that I'm rich, successful—the two prerequisites, if I remember correctly, for any man to be worthwhile in your eyes."

"That's not true!" Memories flooded back and she felt faint.

"No? Then pray tell me why you married Jeremy...."

CATHY WILLIAMS is Trinidadian and was brought up on the twin islands of Trinidad and Tobago. She was awarded a scholarship to study in Britain, and came to Exeter University in 1975 to continue her studies into the great loves of her life: languages and literature. It was there that Cathy met her husband, Richard. Since they married, Cathy has lived in England, originally in the Thames Valley but now in the Midlands. Cathy and Richard have three small daughters.

Books by Cathy Williams

HARLEQUIN PRESENTS
1413—A POWERFUL ATTRACTION
1502—CARIBBEAN DESIRE
1829—BEYOND ALL REASON
1909—ACCIDENTAL MISTRESS

CATHY WILLIAMS

Vengeful Seduction

Harlequin Books

TORONTO • NEW YORK • LONDON
AMSTERDAM • PARIS • SYDNEY • HAMBURG
STOCKHOLM • ATHENS • TOKYO • MILAN
MADRID • WARSAW • BUDAPEST • AUCKLAND

ISBN 0-373-18669-X

VENGEFUL SEDUCTION

First North American Publication 1997.

CHAPTER ONE

WHITE was a dreadful colour. Isobel stared at her reflection in the dressing-table mirror and thought that she would probably never wear it again. It would forever conjure up a feeling of despair.

She began brushing her hair, long dark hair, almost black, which fell down her back in small waves. Sooner or later, she knew, she would have to stop brushing it. She had been up here in her bedroom for well over two hours now, getting dressed, but in reality dodging the inevitable which would be progressing now downstairs.

There was a knock on the door and her mother pushed it open and came inside, smiling. Isobel smiled back. The muscles in her jaw ached from the effort but she had no choice. Brides were supposed to be radiant. It was their hallmark. Whoever heard of a depressed bride?

'I'm nearly ready,' Isobel said, turning around and hearing the rustle of her dress under her. The sleeves felt too tight, restricting almost, and the neckline was too low, but then she had only herself to blame. Her input in choosing the thing had been next to nil. She had allowed her mother to pick the design from a magazine without even glancing at it. It had a top fitted to the waist, from where it fell in a series of chiffon layers down to her calves. She had been measured for it, had tried it on, had nodded at her mother and the seamstress, and she had hardly seen it at all.

Now she realised that she hated it, but then, she thought, she would have hated any bridal dress.

'How do I look?' she asked, standing up, and her mother's smile broadened.

'A picture, darling,' her mother said, with a sheen in her eyes, and Isobel said quickly, firmly,

'No tears—you promised.' Cry, she thought, and I shall burst into tears, and as well as being a depressed bride I shall end up being a depressed bride with mascara streaming down my face. Not an attractive sight.

'But where has my little girl gone?' Mrs Chandler held her daughter's hands and Isobel looked back at her with great love and a growing lump in her throat.

'I'm still here, Mum,' she said. 'You're not losing a daughter; you're gaining a son.' That took quite a bit of doing, and saying it made her feel ever so slightly sick.

'Of course I am, darling,' Mrs Chandler agreed, 'but your dad and I...well... Where have all the years gone? One minute you're a toddler, and now here you are getting married.'

'I had to grow up some time.' It was important to keep her voice light, carefree. It wouldn't do at all to have her parents suspect, even for a moment, that all was not well in Bride City. They would immediately start asking questions, and Isobel couldn't afford for that to happen. She loved them both far too much. She had been the much longed for and only child of a couple who had given up hope of ever having children, and from the day of her birth she had been showered with parental adoration. They had both taken an inordinate delight in everything she had done, said, thought, and Isobel had returned their joy with the same deep love.

'And how do I look?' Mrs Chandler gave a small twirl and Isobel grinned broadly.

'Spectacular.' She did, too. Mrs Chandler was as tall as her daughter was, but fair where Isobel was dark, although they both had the same shade of violet-blue eyes and the same long, thick eyelashes. She was sixty now, but her face was still beautiful, with that amazing bone-structure and that clear, faultless complexion. Parkinson's disease might have tainted her movements, slowed her speech, but it had not diminished her lustre.

'Dad's a lucky man,' Isobel said, and when she thought of her father she had another one of those awful lumps in the back of her throat again.

Mrs Chandler laughed. 'If you could have seen him an hour ago,' she said, 'you wouldn't have described him as a man toppling over under the weight of his good luck. He was scowling rather heavily and trying to squeeze into a dinner-jacket. He insisted that he could still get into the one he wore when we married, and of course he can't. The odd button at the bottom will have to be left undone, but I don't think anyone will notice, do you? All eyes will be on you today, my darling.'

That made Isobel feel almost as sick as she had felt when she had told her mother about not losing a daughter but gaining a son, but she smiled again and tried to look terribly radiant at the thought of that.

'How are the preparations going?' she asked, changing the subject. 'I'm sorry, I should have been helping, but...'

'But nothing. You can't be scurrying around a marquee in your gown, making sure that everything is all right! I know you're nervous—I was awfully nervous on my wedding-day—but there are enough hands downstairs making sure that nothing goes horribly wrong. The caterers have been wonderful, the food looks delicious and the guests have now started trickling in. Your father's holding the fort with Aunt Emma and your cousins. Telling his usual jokes. You know.' She was smiling, her eyes distant and full of affection.

The perfect family unit, Isobel thought. Except nothing was perfect, was it? As she had discovered to her cost.

'Has Jeremy arrived yet?' The question almost strangled her, but she kept right on smiling and looking happy.

'Due shortly.' Mrs Chandler started moving towards the door slowly. 'Darling, I shall have to go and help your father. He'll come and fetch you in a short while, when everything's about to start.' She paused by the door. 'I'm so happy for you, my dear. I know we both said——' she spoke carefully, seriously '—that we were a little disappointed that you didn't finish your university education, but I'm sure, seeing you now, that it's all for the best, and you knew what you were doing.'

She left and Isobel sat on the bed. Now that there was no one in the room, she felt free to stop smiling. She wished that her mother had not brought up the subject of university. She had had to swallow many bitter pills for this marriage, and that had been one of them.

She sighed, and across the room her eyes caught her image looking back at her from the full-length antique pine mirror in the corner of the room. Never mind the years slipping past; that didn't worry her. What worried her was the prospect of the future hurtling towards her.

She slipped on her high, satin shoes. They felt uncomfortable. She was a tall girl and accustomed to wearing flat shoes, but this dress needed high ones. They completed the image, and there was no doubt that the image was a remarkably beautiful one.

Her mother had once told her, rather proudly, that she had been striking even as a baby, and Isobel had never had any reason to doubt that. She only had to look in the nearest mirror to see that those striking looks had never abandoned her.

Her waist-long hair was like finely spun silk, black silk; her skin was ivory-white and her features were perfect. From a very young child she had known admiration, and over the years she had become accustomed to it, even though she felt that her beauty had been a blessing, but in the end it was an irrelevance. Beauty, after all, was transitory, and sometimes, quite frankly, it could be a terrific disadvantage. It opened doors, but the reception waiting at the other end was not always the one you had hoped for.

She walked across to the window and stared down into the huge back garden which her parents had diligently cultivated ever since they had moved into the house. In a few years' time they would have to get a gardener to help them out, or else convert some of the land into pasture, if that were possible, but of course they would defer that until the last possible moment. Her mother had been told at the onset of her illness that her condition would worsen, but Isobel knew that she would continue to tend her garden, lovingly if not as thoroughly.

From here she couldn't see the arriving guests. They would be entering through the front door. Relatives, some of whom she had not seen for a long time; her university friends, who would probably gape and feel dwarfed by the dimensions of her parents' house, because she had never let on just how wealthy her background was; and of course schoolfriends, hers and Jeremy's, shared friends whom they had known from the year dot—just as they had known each other from the year dot.

She gazed down into the garden and attempted to speculate on their reactions to this marriage. Most, she supposed, would see it as a sort of natural conclusion, something expected, but some, her closest friends, had already expressed their horror at the match. She had always been the high achiever, the girl with everything, and they had told her, with varying degrees of tact, just how amazed they were that she was throwing it all away, throwing away a medical degree, for God's sake, to settle down and get married. Naturally she had said nothing. How could she?

Her parents had been disappointed as well, even though they had taken great pains not to condemn her choice. The fact was that they had instilled in her from day one the importance of education, and they had been bewildered when she had arrived home six months previously, sat them down and tonelessly announced her decision to marry Jeremy Baker.

Their immediate concern was that she was pregnant, which, Isobel had thought at the time, had been the only amusing thing about the whole sorry affair.

'It's just that it's all so sudden, darling,' her mother had said, frowning and trying to make sense of the impossible. 'I didn't even think that you and Jeremy were that close. I thought...'

Isobel had known what she had thought, and she had cut in hurriedly, with some nonsense about deciding at last where her heart lay.

'But can't it wait?' her father had asked in a concerned voice, and she hadn't been able to meet his eyes.

'We feel that this is the best way for us,' she had mumbled, and later, when they had gently asked her about her medical degree, she had fudged and muttered something about blood and guts not really being up her street after all.

In the end, they had left it, and her mother had embarked on the wedding preparations with zeal.

Her father was an influential man in the community and strings had been pulled so that everything fell into place with the perfection of an event that could have taken years in the making. Nothing was too small or too great for their daughter, and from the sidelines Isobel had watched and choked back the sickening misery that had threatened to overwhelm her at every turn.

She was consulted on the design for the wedding-invitations, the serviettes, the colours of the flowers which hung in profusion downstairs in the marquee, every conceivable shade of yellow because, her mother had decided, spring was yellow and so the flowers would all represent spring. Frankly, winter would have been more appropriate but she had bitten back the caustic observation and gone along with the general flow.

She began pacing about the room, glancing at the reminders of her childhood which still clung here and there: adventure books which she had devoured in her youth, before biology texts became much more fascinating, a doll which she could remember being given to her as a birthday present from her parents when she was five, a picture of her family which she had done when she was four and which her parents had proudly framed—three figures with odd shapes and stick-like fingers. Her parents had been immensely proud of that picture, but in fact art had been just about the only thing that had eluded her. She had a mind more attuned to the logical.

Ironic, she thought now, that her life, which had been cheerfully pacing towards the most logical conclusion in the world—a degree in the subject she had adored, a career helping people—had petered out into the most irrational ending.

That made her think of Jeremy, and she swallowed down the bitter resentment rising up her throat.

In less than one hour's time she would be his wife, and there was little point in constantly whipping herself with the insanity of it when there was nothing she could possibly do to remedy the situation.

She heard another knock on the door and stiffened in alarm. Surely not her father. Surely not yet. She looked at her watch, which showed that she still had at least forty-five minutes left of freedom, and said, 'Yes? Come in!'

If was probably her mother with some detail that needed sorting out, or else Abigail, the least tactful but closest of her childhood friends, who would no doubt launch into another lecture on the stupidity of the marriage.

'Fine,' she had said when Isobel had told her about Jeremy. 'Throw your life away on that worm! Throw away your hopes of being a doctor! And while you're about it, why don't you fling yourself under the nearest bus as well?' Abigail was studying drama and had cultivated a theatrical way of talking. 'I shall never mention another syllable on the subject again!' But she had continued to expound on the theme whenever they had met, and Isobel assumed that she was about to recommence.

It wasn't Abigail. It wasn't her mother. It was the last person in the world she wanted to face, but face him she did, defiantly across the length of the room.

'So,' he said, strolling into the room and shutting the door behind him, 'the bride is ready.' His voice was sneering, his expression hard and contemptuous.

'What are you doing here?' Isobel asked. Her heart was beating quickly, making her feel giddy and deprived of air. He had always had this sort of dramatic effect on her, as if his presence threw her system into some weird kind of overdrive.

'Didn't you think that I'd turn up?' Lorenzo smiled humourlessly. 'Why, Isobel, my dearest, I'm the best man.'

'Yes.' She licked her dry lips. 'But you should be downstairs, with everyone else.'

What she really meant was that he should be anywhere else, but not here, not in her room. She couldn't bear this game of cruelty he had played ever since he had found out about Jeremy, even though she could understand it.

'I never thought you'd do it,' he bit out, advancing towards her. 'When you told me five months ago what you were planning, I thought that it was a joke, some kind of mad joke.'

'No joke, Lorenzo.'

His hands shot out, grasping her arms, and she winced in pain.

'Why? Why, damn you!'

'I told you...'

'You told me nothing!' He flung her away and walked towards the dressing-table, resting on it with clenched fists.

Isobel followed him, stared at his back, the downbent head, and struggled not to put her arms around him.

Presently he turned around and faced her, his face dark and savage.

'Why are you doing this, Isobel? You're not in love with Jeremy Baker.' There was a sneer in his voice and she answered quickly, to avoid the subject of love.

'How can you speak about him in that tone of voice? I thought he was your friend!'

'We both know him,' Lorenzo bit out. 'He's unstable, reckless. You told me so yourself. Wasn't that one of the reasons that you stopped seeing him, even as a friend, after he went to work for your father? He frightened you. You were glad to be at university.'

'You frighten me too,' she said, 'when you're like this.' They stared at each other. He was furious and his fury, she knew, was given edge by his frustrated bewilderment at the situation. She looked at him, at the whip-hard strength of his body, the dark, sexy good looks which had turned every girl's head at school when he had joined years ago. He had only been sixteen at the time, but already his face had held promise of the powerfully striking man he was to become.

'I am trying to be reasonable, Isobel,' he said in a voice that didn't sound reasonable at all. 'I am trying to work out whether there's something here I'm missing or whether you need to be carted off to the nearest asylum in a strait-jacket.'

His eyes narrowed on her, curiously light eyes that were especially striking given the darkness of his hair and the olive tint of his skin. He was Italian, the son of emigrants who had settled in England, choosing their spot carefully so that their brilliant and gifted only son could be sent to one of the finest private schools in the country. He had easily gained a place on a scholarship and had landed among the students, bright enough but mostly with rich backgrounds, like a leopard in a flock of sheep.

He was different from them all, and he had never seemed to give a damn. He hadn't needed to. His brains were enough to guarantee respect. At sixteen, he possessed a formidable intellect that, it was whispered, out-ranked some of the professors. His mind was brilliant and creative, and his drive to succeed was formidable. Nothing since had changed.

'I know what I'm doing, Lorenzo,' she whispered, looking away to her hands which were clasped in front of her.

'You damn well don't!' he roared, and she glanced nervously at him and then at the door.

'You'll bring everyone rushing up to see what's going on!'

'And I'll tell them exactly what I'm telling you now! That you've gone off your rocker!'

'You don't understand!' she retaliated, and he moved towards her.

'What don't I understand?' He stood in front of her, staring down.

For a second she didn't have a clue what to say. From the start there had been a thread of suspicion underneath his anger at her decision and she realised that her words, spontaneously spoken, had tightened the thread. She couldn't afford for that to happen. He was too clever by half for him to be allowed a glimpse of the truth behind the black farce.

'I care about Jeremy,' she said, not meeting his eyes, and he tilted her chin up in a rough gesture.

'Like hell you do.' His hand moved from her chin to coil into her hair so that she was forced into looking at him. 'There's only one person you care about. Would you like me to prove it to you?' His mouth twisted into a smile but there was nothing gentle in it.

'Lorenzo, don't!'

'Why? Are you frightened?'

'No, of course I'm not frightened!' She tried to laugh but it came out as a choked sound. 'I am going to marry him,' she said, placing her palms on his chest and feeling his masculine energy whip into her like an electric current. 'You may not like the idea, but it's a fact of life and there's no point in trying to do anything about it.'

'You were my lover,' he said in a low, rough voice. 'Were you playing games behind my back with him? Is that it?'

'No!'

'You hardly saw him when you were at university. You hardly went home and weekends were with me.' His brain was ticking, thinking it through, applying the same ruthless intelligence to the enigma as he applied to any problem. 'He could hardly have come up to see you during the week. He wouldn't have been able to wangle the time off from his job.'

'He wrote,' she admitted. It was a small concession and it was true. Jeremy had written.

'You arranged a wedding courtesy of written correspondence?' Lorenzo sneered, and his grasp on her hair tightened. 'Don't make me laugh. You went out with the boy for one term when you were sixteen, yet you set a wedding-date by virtue of a few letters?'

'This is pointless,' she whispered, and anger flooded his face.

'You,' he said grimly, 'have been mine since you were sixteen. You are twenty now and we have been lovers for over a year. Jeremy has never been a part of that picture. You have always belonged to me.'

The words invaded her mind and threw up images of Lorenzo, his strong arms wrapped around her, his mouth exploring her body. He had been her first and only lover.

'I belong to myself,' she muttered, trying to wriggle free.

'Tell me that you're in love with him,' Lorenzo murmured savagely in her ear. 'Let me hear you say it.'

He was so close to her that she could feel his heart beating, smell the rough sweetness of his skin. Ever since she had known that she would marry Jeremy, she had avoided Lorenzo Cicolla like the plague, because his proximity was the one thing she had feared most and, standing here, she knew that she had been right.

'You can't, can you?' he taunted. 'Then why? Has he threatened you? Answer me!'

'Of course not,' she heard herself say quickly, too quickly. 'I've known him since we were children. We played together. We had the same set of friends.'

'I played marbles with a girl called Francesca when I was ten but that didn't automatically mean that we were destined for each other, for God's sake! Anyway, you're talking in the past tense. The past tense is history.'

'History makes us!'

'You forget, I know him well too. Well enough to know that he can be dangerous. He has always taken risks, stupid risks, and the only reason he's got away with them is because his parents have had the money to bail him out every time.'

'He holds down a job!'

'That means nothing.'

'Why are you his best man if you hate him so much?' she asked bitterly. Why are you? Why did you have to be here?

'Don't you know? He offered it as a challenge, Isobel, and I never refuse a challenge.'

'You're as bad as he is.'

'My intelligence outstrips his,' he said in a hard, controlled voice. 'Any risks I take are born from cool calculation. Jeremy saw me as a threat the minute I set foot in that school and when he discovered that I couldn't be bullied into taking his orders, he did the next best thing. He decided to befriend me, and frankly I didn't care one way or the other. But don't you know that underneath the friendship there has always been an undercurrent of envy and resentment?'

'I know,' Isobel muttered. 'But he did like you.'

'He respected me.' Lorenzo said this without a trace of vanity. 'When he asked me to be his best man, we both knew the reason. The reason was you.'

She turned away, not wanting to hear any more. Everything he said was tearing her apart.

'You were the prize draw,' he mocked. 'You have always been the prize draw. In this little, tight-knit community, you were the light that outshone the rest. You dazzled everyone. You were the greatest trophy.'

'Where is this getting us, Lorenzo?' she asked, doing her utmost to keep the misery out of her voice.

'You're catapulting yourself headlong into disaster,' he grated, a dull red flush spreading over his cheeks. 'There is still time to get out of its path.'

This, she knew, was the closest he would ever get to begging, and it made every bone in her body ache with the craving to do just what he asked.

Everything he had said about Jeremy was true. Jeremy had been obsessed with her. He had singled her out and it had never really occurred to him that his privileged background, which had bought him everything, couldn't similarly buy him her. He had proposed to her when she was sixteen, still at school, while he had been at university, four years her senior. She had laughed. Now the joke was on her.

'I will marry Jeremy——' she looked at her watch '—in less than thirty minutes' time,' she said in a whisper, 'and that's all there is to it.'

His lips tightened and his expression changed subtly from anger to contempt. She didn't know which she hated more.

'I never took you for a coward or a fool, Isobel Chandler, but I'm rapidly revising my opinion.'

'People are more complex than you give them credit for,' she said in a low voice.

'What are you trying to say to me?' His eyes glinted and the sun, streaming in behind him through the large bay window, gave him a brooding, dangerous air that frightened and excited her. He had always frightened and excited her, she realised. He had walked into that school and she had been open-mouthed. She and every other girl in the class. They had been a group hesitatingly crossing the dividing line between childhood and adulthood, realising with an uncertain thrill that boys were not quite as uninteresting as they had once assumed. Lorenzo Cicolla with his bronzed skin and his black hair, four years older but vastly more mature than the other boys of his own age, had captivated their imagination. They had giggled from the sidelines, observed him from the distance with the blushing innocence of youth.

The fact that he had not looked at her, at any of them, even with the mildest of curiosity, had only added to his appeal. In fact, it was only when she was sixteen, ironically through Jeremy, that they had struck up a tentative friendship and he had admitted, with amusement at her reaction, that he had always noticed her. He might have been young, but he had already cultivated the dark, intense composure that had hardened as he got older.

'I'm not trying to say anything.'

'No? Why do I get the impression that you're talking in riddles?'

'I have no idea.' She shrugged but her hands were trembling, and she quickly stuck them behind her back and clasped them together.

'What did those letters say?'

She gave him a blank look, and then realised what he was talking about. She might have guessed that he would not have left for too long her unwary admission that Jeremy had written to her. There had only been one letter, but she wasn't going to tell him that.

'This and that,' she muttered uncomfortably. 'Why are we going through this?'

'Be more specific.'

'I can't. I don't remember.'

'Ah.' His face cleared and he shot her a cruel, cold look. 'You can't remember what was said in those letters, yet you still decided to marry the man.'

'No! You don't understand! You're putting words into my mouth,' she said in confusion.

'Can you blame me, dammit?' He gripped her and his eyes were so ferocious that she was terrified that he would do something awful, shake her until she came apart. She opened her mouth to protest and his lips met hers in a kiss that was fuelled by anger.

Isobel whimpered and pushed at him and eventually he stood back and stared down at her.

'What's the matter, Isobel?' he asked, his mouth twisting. 'Can't you bear to bid a fond farewell to your lover?'

'Stop it!' she moaned. She felt close to tears. When she had first told him about Jeremy, he had been angry, but proud. Too proud to question. He had stormed out of her university flat and had not returned. Time had obviously worked on his fury, stoking it. It was a strange, back-handed compliment to her, but one she would rather have avoided.

'Why?' he snarled.

'You know why! I belong to Jeremy now. It's just the way it is.'

He turned away abruptly, but not before she caught the hatred that her remark had aroused. She realised, because she knew him so well, that she had not phrased her heated reply in the most tactful way possible, but just then, with her passions threatening to soar out of control, she had had to say something that would deflect him from realising how powerful his effect on her still was.

She made a stilted move towards him, then there was a knock on the door and she sprang back as though she had been burned.

It was her father. He came into the room and gave them a puzzled look, in answer to which Lorenzo said, in a normal voice, as though nothing had happened between them, 'Just wishing the bride good luck. I doubt I shall see much of her once the wedding is under way, and we've known each other for so long and——' he faced her with a smile even though his eyes were as hard as diamonds '—so well, that I thought a private last farewell would be in order.'

Her father came into the room, oblivious to the undercurrents, and nodded with genial understanding.

'Quite understand, my dear fellow,' he said warmly. He had always liked Lorenzo. 'Lucky chap, getting this beautiful daughter of mine.'

Lorenzo looked at her with icy courtesy. 'I don't know whether luck had a great part to play in it. Love, perhaps, wouldn't you say, Isobel?'

'Yes, of course,' she said, reaching out to hold her father's hand. She couldn't look at Lorenzo. That would have been a Herculean feat quite beyond her just at that moment.

'Well, dear girl, luck or love doesn't change the fact that your time has come.' Her father cleared his throat and patted her hand and she thought how true his unwitting choice of expression was. 'I hope you're not feeling too dicky. I need your support or else I might just collapse with nerves before we make it to the altar.' He turned to Lorenzo with a grin. 'Wait until you're my age and your daughter is about to marry. You'll soon discover what nerves are all about. I've addressed enough roomfuls of people, but I've never felt this fraught before.' He rested his hand on his stomach. 'Viola says that it's indigestion caused by trying to fit my frame into this outfit. Mothers! Don't know a thing.' His voice held the same level of tender affection when he spoke of his wife as hers did when she spoke of him.

'Try telling them that,' Lorenzo said drily. 'My mama has always maintained that she rules the roost, which, of course, she does.' They both laughed at this and Isobel forced her lips into a mimicry of a smile.

'Well, my dear, shall we go down and make our grand entrance?' He looked at Lorenzo. 'Jeremy has been looking for you. Told him I didn't know whether you'd arrived or not. Didn't know that you were up here, paying your last respects, so to speak.' He had moved towards the door, his mind already on the task ahead, and he missed their various reactions to Jeremy's name.

Isobel clutched his hand and they stood aside so that Lorenzo could leave first, which he did, taking the steps two at a time. She heard his footsteps fading along the marble hallway and felt a dreadful sense of resignation, as if she had aged fifty years in the space of half an hour.

The wedding-ceremony and the reception were both being held in the massive yellow and white marquee, which had been connected to the back doors. She wouldn't even have the impersonal, imposing view of the inside of a church to fall back on. No, in the marquee they would all be standing close together, too close. Her mother had thought it a wonderful idea, and with cheerful apathy Isobel had agreed. Now she wished that she hadn't.

She and her father walked sedately down the winding staircase, through the hallway, into the grand apricot and green drawing-room, which had efficiently been cleared of empty glasses and full ashtrays by some of the hired help, and finally through the open French doors and into the marquee, and the further they progressed, the stiffer Isobel felt.

By the time they reached the marquee, and all eyes swivelled in their direction, she felt dead inside. She stared straight ahead, not meeting anyone's eye, least of all her dissenting clique of friends who had all, naturally, convened in the front row. Out of the corner of her eye she spotted Abigail—straight blonde hair, firm features, disapproving eyes.

Ahead she saw Lorenzo, dark and deadly and staring at her with a veiled contempt which only she would recognise. And beyond him Jeremy, dear, obsessed Jeremy, whose fate would now be entwined with hers forever.

the morning, and the lumber further prepared, the ability woke up.

In this time they reached the province, and all over forwarded in their direction, she had dead fields. She stared straight and the hesitating clatter an eye, took of all the that the clatter in prospect who had fill, nat-

CHAPTER TWO

THE accountant was saying something. Isobel looked at him and tried to focus her mind on what was happening. Next to her, her mother sat like a statue on the flowered upright chair, leaning forward slightly, her body stiff as board, her face set in lines of pain. She had been like this for the past three months. Her body moved, her mouth spoke, but the soul had gone out of her.

'It'll take time,' Richard Adams had told Isobel in the privacy of the surgery. 'She'll go through all those emotions of anger, despair, shock, disbelief, but she's strong enough to pull through. In time.'

Isobel looked at the unmoving figure with distress, and wondered whether her mother's strength hadn't been over-exaggerated.

'I advise you strongly to sell,' the accountant was saying, flicking through his paperwork.

'Sell?' Isobel shot him a dazed look, and he shook his head impatiently. He was a small man, balding, with quick, darting eyes and a manner that implied constant nervous movement. He was efficient, though. He and his team of two had run through her father's accounts like torpedoes—dispassionately, ruthlessly.

'Your father's company has its head above water at the moment,' Mr Clark said, his fingers twitching over the paperwork. 'But only just. There has been some shocking mismanagement over the past few years. Not,' he added hurriedly, seeing Mrs Chandler's face turn towards him in sad, pained accusation, 'because of anything Mr Chandler did. After all, he had virtually

24

resigned by the time . . . Yes, well, we often find that this is a problem in family firms. They employ friends, and there's altogether too much trust and too little ruthlessness. It shows in the company accounts eventually.' He sat back, crossed his legs, linked his fingers together on his lap, and fixed them with what was, for him, a relatively serene stare.

'The fact of the matter is that the company has been left jointly to you both, but it would be madness to continue running it keeping on some of the management who are currently employed there. In no time at all it would cease to be a going concern, and then if you did decide to sell it would fetch you next to nothing. It would become the victim of a predator looking for a dying company to dissect. Simple as that.'

Isobel looked at her mother and said gently, 'You go, Mum. You look tired.'

Mrs Chandler forced a smile on to her face. 'No, of course not, darling. After all, this affects me as well.' She made a small, despairing gesture with her hands and lapsed back into silence.

'I have a prospective buyer already,' Mr Clark said bluntly, 'and I suggest that you give very serious thought to selling to him. He has offered an absurdly generous price. You and your mother could retire millionaires.'

That was not a well-chosen remark. Mrs Chandler looked away with tear-filled eyes and said in a choked voice, 'The money means nothing at all to me, to us. It won't bring David back, will it? Or. . .' She couldn't go on. She began to sob quietly, resting her forehead in her hands, and Isobel hurried over to her side and wrapped her arms around her. She had hardly had time herself to grieve. She had had to carry her mother through her grief; she had had to be strong for her.

She made a silent, brushing gesture over her mother's head to Mr Clark, who awkwardly rose to his feet, cleared his throat and muttered a belated, red-faced apology.

'Wait in the hall for me, Mr Clark,' Isobel said briefly, and he nodded and left noiselessly through the drawing-room door.

'I'm sorry, my darling,' Mrs Chandler said, 'I know I should be pulling myself together.' She raised her red eyes to Isobel, who tried to maintain a strong, re-assuring face when she felt like breaking up inside. 'You poor love.' She managed a watery smile which made Isobel feel worse. 'I've been no comfort to you, have I?'

'You always are. Whatever you do.'

'Your loss has been double,' she sighed, and then said finally, 'Run along, darling, see what Mr Clark suggests. I'll leave it all to you.'

Isobel hesitated, but only for a moment. Things needed to be sorted out. The issues which Mr Clark had raised left no time for grief. Life continued to march on, demanding involvement. It had no respect for death.

Mr Clark was waiting patiently in the hall when Isobel went out to join him. She ushered him through to the kitchen, poured him some coffee, which he accepted with alacrity, and then took the chair facing him across the kitchen table.

'Who is the buyer, Mr Clark?' she asked, coming to the point, and he relaxed. Displays of emotion, she suspected, made him uneasy. He was only at home when discussing work.

'I have been dealing with a Mr Squires from London,' he said, sipping his coffee. 'There have, in fact, been several poachers waiting on the sidelines. Your father's business may have been mismanaged, but it still has considerable potential and an impressive client portfolio.'

'That being the case, what is there to stop me from running the business myself?'

'Knowledge.' He carefully placed the cup on the saucer, fixed her with those quick eyes, and said with clipped certainty, 'Good intentions won't make a success out of a business. Most of the hierarchy in your father's firm will have to be sacked. Many of them are friends of the family. Could you do that? Your training, if you don't mind my pointing it out, is not financial. Of course, I can only advise, but keeping the company going under your own auspices, merely for sentimental reasons, is not going to do much good. In the end, if it dissolves, you will see the loss of a great many more jobs than those which will be lost should you sell now.'

Isobel thought about that. What he said made sense. Everything he had said over the past few weeks made sense. Mr Clark, it had to be faced, was an eminently sensible man.

'When,' she asked, 'will you need my answer?'

'The sooner the better.'

She nodded and stood up, and he followed suit, collecting his various files and stacking them into his briefcase. He had come well-prepared. Statistics had been shown her, profit and loss columns had been methodically pointed out, budgets analysed, and he had been right: she knew very little about finance. In time, she was sure, she could get to grips with it, but 'in time' might not be soon enough, and she knew that it would have broken her father's heart to witness the dissolution of his beloved company. Better for it to carry on in a different form. Wasn't it?

She showed Mr Clark out, looked in on her mother, who had fallen into a fitful sleep on the chair, and then retreated to the library to think.

It was so hard being strong, she thought wearily. Decisions had to be made and her mother, she knew, was in no fit state to make them.

Isobel sat back in the leather swivel chair and closed her eyes. Memories were the worst. Her father sitting her on his knee when she was a child, going for walks with her, patiently telling her about the various plants and trees in the garden.

She didn't sob like her mother. The tears squeezed themselves out, but she didn't brush them away. They fell on to her hands, on her lap, her dress.

That dreamlike feeling of unreality which had first dogged her had gone. Now she could think of the policeman at the door, breaking the news to them that there had been a car accident, that both occupants had been killed outright, without trying to convince herself that she would wake up at any moment and find that it had only been a terrible nightmare.

Jeremy had been at the wheel of the Jaguar. He had been overtaking another car and had been hit by an oncoming lorry. He had been over the limit.

She had tried very hard, but bitterness towards him had overlaid any pain she might have felt. He had ruined her life.

The following morning she telephoned Mr Clark and told him to go ahead with the sale of the company.

'You have my trust in this matter, Mr Clark,' she said down the line. 'I will sign whatever needs signing, but I want no involvement beyond that.'

Her mother was out for the day, taken under wing by Jeremy's mother, who had been distraught at the funeral but over the past weeks had been a source of strength to Mrs Chandler. They were going to have tea in one of the coffee-shops in the village.

That left Isobel on her own, and she made her way back to her own house. Ever since the accident she had been living with her mother, and it had been something of a relief.

The house she had shared with Jeremy, even after four years of marriage, had never felt like a home. She had looked after the gardens, arranged flowers in vases, hung paintings, but it still remained a stiff, empty shell. A house could never become a home without love to fill it, and love was something that had been conspicuous by its absence.

She pushed open the front door, stooped down to collect the dribs and drabs of mail, and then, unemotionally, she resumed her sporadic job of packing Jeremy's clothes into boxes which she had retrieved from the attic. She should have done it sooner, weeks ago, but time had flown past so quickly.

Suits, ties, trousers, jumpers, shirts. She would give them all to charity.

It had all been so pointless. She could remember being twenty, being in love, Lorenzo. Her throat constricted. Of course that had been another life, and she had got over him. Time healed everything; that much was true.

She hadn't even had the reminder of his mother, because Mrs Cicolla had emigrated to America to be with her son three years previously.

She could still remember that dead, sickly feeling that had spread over her when he had announced at the wedding, not to her but to her parents, that he had decided to emigrate.

'Within a fortnight,' he had said casually, his hand in his pocket, his eyes not looking at her at all, eliminating her from his life in one fell swoop. Ex-lover with another man's ring on her finger. No longer worth so much as token politeness.

That had been four years ago, but the memory was as clear as if it had been only yesterday, only a few hours ago.

She heard the buzz of the doorbell and ran down the stairs to answer it. Abigail. Isobel's face broke into a smile of pure joy. She hadn't seen Abigail, apart from briefly at the funeral three months ago.

'I tried your mum's house first,' Abigail said, coming inside, 'and when there was no reply, I thought that you might be here.' She looked sympathetically at Isobel. 'Do you need a hand with anything?'

They went upstairs and continued boxing the clothes, chatting. Abigail's status, in the space of only a few years, had reached mammoth proportions. She was in the newspapers all the time, her movements shadowed and faithfully, or unfaithfully, reported back on.

'How's your mum coping?' she asked casually, and Isobel paused to look at her.

'Not very well,' she answered truthfully. 'She seems to have retreated into herself.'

'It's understandable.'

'She doesn't even venture out into the garden. She says every blade of grass reminds her of him.'

Abigail didn't say anything for a while. 'And you, Izzy?' She looked away and busied herself with stuffing more clothes into boxes. Jeremy had had a lot of clothes. He had liked dressing the part of the wealthy landowner.

'He's in my mind,' Isobel said in a low voice.

'And Jeremy?'

Isobel stood up, dusted herself down and replied shortly, 'You know that he caused the accident. The coroner told me that in privacy. I asked him if he could withhold the information from his parents, and from Mum.'

'You always hated him, didn't you?'

'No.' Isobel thought about it, for the first time putting into words what had never been said before. 'He trapped me into marriage, and please don't ask me how or why.' Those papers. She frowned. Where were they? He must have hidden them somewhere. They could not have vanished into thin air. Oh, no. He would never have been so careless as to misplace them—after all, they were the stick to be waved over her if ever she thought of desertion. 'Of course I hated him to start with, but you can't hate forever. It's too tiring. After a while, the instinct for self-preservation takes over or else you would just go mad.' She shrugged and they went down to the kitchen to have some coffee.

It helped having someone to talk to. It made her co-ordinate her thoughts, and Isobel found herself telling Abigail about Mr Clark's offer, what she intended to do with her house, her job.

'I might even contemplate finding out whether I can't complete some kind of medical course, take it up,' she said, blushing. 'Richard thinks it's a good idea.'

'Richard?' Abigail's eyebrows quirked. 'Dr Adams, you mean?'

'He's very encouraging.'

'And, so that's how the land lies.'

'Of course not!' Isobel laughed. 'You and that dramatic mind of yours! Richard and I are simply good friends. He's been kind to me over the years.'

And they left it at that. Abigail departed late that evening and Isobel returned to find her mother in better spirits than she had been for weeks.

'Emily is helping me to put everything in perspective, the dear woman,' she said, sipping tea and picking bits of salad from her plate like a choosy bird deliberating over which morsels to consume. 'David is gone, and hiding myself away isn't going to change that. I've spent too long hiding. I want to start thinking about to-morrow. What did Mr Clark say?'

So Isobel told her, and the following morning, by some uncanny coincidence, he telephoned to inform her that the purchaser had arrived and would she come down to his offices on the High Street to sign some bits of paper.

Isobel dressed carefully for the occasion. A sober grey wool suit, because the chill of autumn was in the air, her pearls, cream-coloured shoes.

She looked in the mirror and saw the reflection of a twenty-four-year-old woman, nearly twenty-five, who, in the midst of loss, now found herself on the brink of freedom for the first time in four long years.

She smiled, and the image smiled back, showing her what she hadn't seen for a very long time. The same stunning face, but with the black hair trimmed to a bob, a tall, lithe body, eyes that were a little sad, as though they had seen too much.

She swept out of the house, feeling better than she had done for a while, and arrived at Mr Clark's offices well in time.

Mr Squires wasn't there. Isobel drank coffee, made small talk to the accountant, and began to feel slightly annoyed that she was being kept waiting. Hadn't this man heard of common politeness?

She glanced at her watch and caught Mr Clark's eye. He was looking worriedly at his own watch. Presently he stood up, and said that he would go and have a look to see what had happened to the gentleman in question.

'Perhaps he's lost,' he volunteered politely, to which she was tempted to point out that he could only have found himself lost in a town the size of theirs if he was a mental incompetent, in which case was she really doing the right thing by selling him her father's company?

He vanished out of the room and ten minutes later, having quietly convinced herself that Mr Squires, the invisible man, was definitely not in the running as a prospective buyer for the company, she heard the door being pushed open.

She automatically looked around.

The shock she felt on seeing Lorenzo Cicolla standing in the doorway was as great as if she had looked out of the window and casually seen a mushroom cloud hanging over the town, announcing nuclear war.

He strolled into the room, not taking his eyes off her face, and she stood up, drained of colour. She was shaking, trembling like a leaf, like someone who had seen a ghost. Her mind felt as though it was being bombarded by so many images, so many feelings, that any minute it would shut down from overload.

'Lorenzo Cicolla! What are you doing here? I'm expecting a Mr Squires—he should be here any moment. You're not Mr Squires,' was all she managed to get out, which was an achievement since her vocal cords appeared to have deserted her.

She had never expected to see Lorenzo Cicolla again. He had been the stick of dynamite thrown into her young life, blowing it to pieces, and those pieces had never successfully been put together again. But still, she had relegated him to the past. She had locked that haunting image into a safe room and she had tried damned hard never to open the door.

What was he doing here?

'No,' Lorenzo agreed smoothly, unsmiling, his pale eyes assessing her with arrogant thoroughness. 'I'm not, am I?'

He sat down in the chair next to her and crossed his legs, and she wished desperately that she could stop staring but she couldn't. It had been a long time.

The passage of time showed itself in the tiny lines by his eyes and mouth, the hardness of his features, but apart from that she might have been staring at the Lorenzo of old. He had the same terrifying sex-appeal, the same dark, brooding good looks.

'I apologise for staring,' Isobel said stiltedly, 'but I can't believe that it's really you, sitting there.' She threw him a tentative smile which met with a blank wall.

'I was sorry to hear about your father,' he said abruptly, looking away. 'I'm afraid the news was rather late in reaching me.'

'Thank you. Yes. It was a tragic accident.' Platitudes were becoming easier to mouth. No one felt comfortable with raw emotion and she had learned to control her responses to the polite condolences of neighbours and people in the village.

'And of course, Jeremy.'

'Thank you. Of course.'

'What exactly happened?'

She shrugged and her fingers nervously plucked her wool skirt. 'The car went out of control. There was a lorry coming in the opposite direction. Jeremy was killed outright. My father——' she paused and took a deep, stabilising breath '—died in the ambulance.'

'How is your mother coping with it?'

'Why are you here?' It was easier to ask that now that she had recovered some of her self-control.

He smiled coolly, and she could see dislike and contempt lurking beneath the surface. It made her blood run cold. 'Surely we aren't yet finished with the preliminaries, are we, Isobel? It's been years—four years to be precise.'

'Yes. I know. You left this town without a backward glance, Lorenzo.' Her heart was still beating irregularly and she had the strangest feeling of having stepped into a mad, nonsensical world, like Alice in Wonderland. One blink and it would all disappear. She blinked but nothing disappeared, not even the breathless tension gripping her lungs, making breathing laborious and difficult.

He shrugged. 'I always knew that I would return, when the time was right.'

'And why is the time right now?'

'Because, my dear, I am about to buy your father's company.'

'You!' She looked at him in stunned silence. 'But Mr Clark said... He told me...'

'That Mr Squires was interested. Yes. Mr Squires was interested, on my behalf.'

She stood up and began pacing the room, while Lorenzo remained where he was, watching her, his face revealing nothing.

'You can't be serious,' she said at last, standing in front of him but not too close, because something about him was vaguely menacing. Had this been the same man who had fired her passions once upon a time? Surely not!

'I have never been more serious about anything in my entire life.'

'But why?'

His lips thinned. 'Because I like the beauty of the wheel that turns full circle.'

'Revenge, Lorenzo?' she whispered incredulously.

'Oh, revenge is too strong a word.'

'Then why my father's company?'

'It poses an interesting challenge,' he drawled, but the lazy cruelty was still there in his voice and in the rigid lines of his face.

'And the fact that my father owned it has nothing to do with it?'

'A little, I suppose.' He shrugged dismissively, although his eyes never left her face, not for a second. 'Besides, I've become tired of city life. Chicago has lost its appeal. It will be nice returning here for a while.'

'You'll be coming back *here* to live?'

'But of course. What else did you expect?'

Not that. Anything but that, Isobel thought. Four years ago they had parted in anger and bitterness. Words had been spoken, things said... She stifled the memory of her disastrous wedding-day, that awful confrontation in the garden, before he had walked out of her life forever. Had he simply been biding his time until an opportunity such as this arose, or had the death of Jeremy and her father rekindled buried feelings of anger?

'You don't look too thrilled with the prospect,' he said, eyebrows raised, his mouth curling with a hint of cynicism.

'Of course, it will be nice to see you...' Her voice trailed off.

'Don't lie, Isobel. Your face is too transparent.'

She flushed angrily. 'What do you want me to say? You walk back into town after four years and announce that you plan on settling here, but there's nothing pleasant about the announcement, is there? You're not planning on settling here for the good of the community. You're planning on settling here because you have a chance to settle old scores.' She looked at him bitterly. 'Aren't we both too old for this?'

He banged his fist on the table with such force that Isobel jumped and looked at him warily. He wasn't going to get violent, was he? Then she laughed nervously to herself. Of course not. How could he in such a public place? Besides, she knew Lorenzo. He had never been a man given to displays of violence.

You don't know him now, though, a little voice warned. People change. The face she was staring at with apprehension was the face of a stranger, a dark, menacing stranger.

'Too old?' he sneered. 'Too old to forget the past, Isobel?'

'What happened happened a long time ago...' She glanced at the door and he followed the line of her eyes with a cold smile.

'Mr Clark has been told to wait until I am ready.'

'What?'

'I informed him that there were things I wanted to discuss with you in private.'

'The sale of my father's business isn't a private matter,' she began, but that wasn't the object of his discussion, was it? 'Can't we put the past behind us? We can be friends...'

'Friends?' He almost laughed at that, his eyebrows shooting up in an expression of contempt that made her burn. 'I'm sure you'd like nothing better, Isobel.'

'What does that mean?'

'Oh, only that I'm here, rich and successful—the two prerequisites, if I remember correctly, for any man to be worthwhile in your eyes.'

'That's not true!' More memories flooded back and she felt faint.

'No?' He relaxed back in the swivel chair and folded his hands on his lap. 'Then pray tell me why you married Jeremy, and why you stayed married to him for four long years? Your precious status quo. You needed it so badly that you sacrificed your life for it.'

Isobel stood up, trembling, white. 'I don't have to remain here and listen to this,' she said curtly, turning towards the door.

'Sit back down!'

She looked at him over her shoulder. 'You don't give me orders, Lorenzo Cicolla!'

'Sit back down!' he roared, and she hastily sat back down, wondering whether his bellow wouldn't bring Mr Clark scurrying back into his office. But no one came.

'Now you listen to me,' he said, and his voice was the voice of a man with steel running through his veins. He leaned forward. 'Your father's company needs a buyer if it's to survive in one piece.'

'I can choose my buyer,' she said coldly, and he laughed under his breath.

'Really?'

'Mr Clark told me that there are several offers in the pipeline.'

'No offers, Isobel.'

'But...'

'I am the only bidder. Without me, your father's company will quickly fall into ruin. It's a wonder that it hasn't before now. If it falls into ruin, my darling, it will be sold off in bits and pieces to the highest bidders and you will watch your father's handiwork go down the drain. Do you want that?'

Isobel looked at him with dislike. He was enjoying this. He was enjoying her discomfort, enjoying watching her in a position of helpless subservience. How could she ever have felt love for this man? He was a sadist.

She could, she knew, explain, after all these years, why she had married Jeremy, but if he was hell-bent on revenge, then might not that confession give him the ammunition he needed? It was a chance she could not take. Her father was dead. He was beyond pain. But her mother was still alive, ill, vulnerable, and already buffeted by enough misfortune.

Besides, and she might as well face it, the Lorenzo Cicolla she had known, the man who had once, so long ago that she could scarcely recall, made love to her, laughed with her, was gone. This was someone else. Someone she no longer understood.

'What do you gain from all this, Lorenzo?' she asked with quiet desperation.

'Passing satisfaction,' he said, his lips twisting, and she clenched her fists uselessly at her sides.

'At my expense.'

'Is that so difficult to understand?' He smiled with sarcasm.

'Why fight when we can——?'

'Make love?'

Colour swept into her face. She could feel it burning through her, making her perspire lightly, and the hairs on the back of her neck stand on end.

'When we can be friends...' she whispered.

He was looking at her, his eyes roving insolently over her body. 'A tempting thought,' he said silkily. 'You're still a beautiful woman. More so. Time has put character into your face. But no, I think I can resist you.' He was smiling again, that cool smile that made her want to hit him. 'I don't think I could stomach the thought that your friendship had only been offered because I am now rich enough to pay the right price.'

'You're despicable.'

That brought an angry flush to his face. 'Your marriage to Jeremy Baker was hardly what I would call a noble gesture, Isobel. Or perhaps it's simply my peasant mind that persists in thinking in such inconvenient black and white terms.'

Isobel looked at him from under her lashes. Peasant? Hardly. He might have come from the wrong side of the tracks, as Jeremy had been fond of saying whenever his name cropped up, but no one looking at him would ever have guessed that. Sitting there, in his expensive tailored suit, he looked what he was: wealthy, sophisticated, ruthless.

'Why didn't you stay in America?' It was more the agonised voicing of a private thought than a question demanding an answer.

'I told you. I lost interest in the bright lights.'

She doubted that. He had not 'lost interest' in the bright lights. He had merely decided that there was a bigger, more fulfilling challenge waiting for him here.

He would initially have been drawn to her father's company because it probably fell into the realms of what he was accustomed to dealing with. The actual ownership was, she suspected, added spice.

'How did you find out about...?'

'It was reported in the financial news,' Lorenzo answered. 'Bob Squires, my man in London, faxed me the article. He thought that I might find the coincidence amusing as well as a possibility for take-over. Of course, he doesn't know a great deal about my personal life, but he did know where I had lived in my youth.'

'I see. And does anyone know much about your personal life, Lorenzo?' she asked bitterly, and was rewarded with a look of angry discomfort. It only lasted seconds but in that time she had a fleeting glimpse of something lying beneath the cold, arrogant exterior.

'I dislike people who try to pry into what's no business of theirs.' He stood up abruptly and gazed out of the window, his back to her.

'What a lonely life you must have led all these years,' she murmured, and he spun around to face her, his eyes savage and mocking.

'I hardly think that you're someone qualified to pass judgement on the quality of other people's lives,' he said tersely. 'Marriage for money, quite frankly, makes me sick. Were you *ever* happy, Isobel? When the socialising was over and there were just the two of you left in your big, expensive, empty house?'

She looked away, agitated, and said nothing.

'I thought not.' He had regained his composure but he didn't sit back down. He prowled restlessly around the room, staring at her, and she felt like a trapped rabbit, knowing that whatever he said she would lose because she was incapable of justifying her past.

'If you want me to sign papers,' she said stiffly, 'I shall do so. If not, I'm leaving.'

'You'll leave when I'm ready for you to leave.'

She met his cool grey eyes with anger. 'I don't work for you, Lorenzo. You're not my boss! I'm prepared to sell my father's company to you because the move was recommended by Mr Clark, but beyond that I want nothing to do with you!'

'Now there's a thought,' he murmured, moving behind her and resting his hands on either side of her chair. Her body froze. She wanted nothing to do with him but his sexuality, which had held her in its snare all those years ago, was as powerful as ever. She could feel it emanating from him, from those strong arms only inches away from her.

'What are you talking about?' she asked, licking her lips nervously.

'You could,' he murmured, 'always work for me. Wouldn't that be fun?'

'No,' Isobel muttered in a strangled voice. She wanted badly to move but she was afraid, she realised, of touching him.

'No,' he agreed, 'perhaps it wouldn't be. Or perhaps it wouldn't be enough.' The grey eyes swept over her, the eyes of a predator that had trapped its quarry and was lazily contemplating what course of action to take next.

'What do you mean? What are you talking about?' Her voice had risen a pitch higher.

'The fate of your father's company is in my hands, Isobel. Without me, everything he spent a lifetime working for will vanish like a puff of smoke.' He smiled as though the thought afforded him immense satisfaction.

Isobel looked at him in frozen shock.

'Another buyer can be found,' she persisted weakly.

'I think not.' Another smile, and she felt a quiver of confused alarm.

'No...' He strolled lazily to the window, his hands in his pockets, and turned to face her. 'I have returned, Isobel, and this time I am calling the shots. I will have you, Isobel Chandler, and then, when I tire of you, I shall cast you aside.'

'And you said that you didn't want revenge?' There was a dangerous electricity in the air.

He contemplated her coldly.

'Revenge. Such a basic word. But maybe you're right. Maybe revenge is the only thing that can satisfy me. I will put a ring on your finger and you will be mine for however long I want you. In return, I will salvage your father's company.'

CHAPTER THREE

'NEVER!' Shock made her start back and she found that her hands were gripping the arms of the chair. 'You're mad!'

'Why?' His voice was controlled, but whip-hard, and his eyes pierced into her with a venom that made her cringe.

'I can't believe that you would go to such lengths, Lorenzo... The past is over and done with...'

'It is *never* over and done with. Do you understand me? It has festered inside me and now that I have my opportunity to do something about it, I damn well will.'

'I will never marry you!' He hated her. It was as simple as that. Dislike, contempt, wounded male pride, those were never strong enough to describe what he felt towards her. She could see that now, and she knew with utmost finality that she could never unburden her secret to him. If he was prepared to marry her simply to sate his desire for revenge, then how could she ever trust him?

'You will do precisely what I say, Isobel, because you have no choice.'

'Never! Do you understand, Lorenzo Cicolla? Never, never, never!' She stood up because she was too agitated to sit down, but she didn't walk towards the door. Something in the room kept her rooted to the spot.

'Why ever not, my dear?' he asked with aggravatingly exaggerated politeness. He was standing behind the desk, towering over her. 'In fact, I have no idea how you could resist such a charming proposition. After all, you'll be able to maintain your status quo; you'll have your wealthy lifestyle. If I recall correctly, those were the things that meant so much more to you than I ever did.' There was no fondness in his voice as he recalled their shared past, no softening in his features. If anything his face hardened, and she shivered.

'Believe what you will,' she muttered, looking away, and he moved around the desk so swiftly that before she realised it he was standing next to her. He curled his fingers into her hair and dragged her face to his.

Her heart began to beat, to pound, and she licked her lips nervously. She would never marry him, but some primitive response to his masculinity unfurled deep within her and her eyes widened in shock and an instinctive response to retreat as quickly as she could.

But retreat was impossible. His grip was like a vice. She stood completely still and tried to stifle the treacherous warmth rushing through her.

'Believe what I will, Isobel?' he asked, his lips curling. 'Surely you mean, believe what you told me? Told me four years ago?'

She didn't answer. Was there a way to answer the unanswerable?

The memories sprang up at her like monsters rushing out from the dark. The wedding-day, gloriously sunny, a still, fine spring day that had felt more like summer. Jeremy, looking at her with satisfaction, knowing that he now owned her.

She had been surprised and taken aback when Lorenzo had remained for the reception. She had thought that he would take the first opportunity to leave a situation which he despised, but a part of her realised that he would remain because to leave would be to throw in his hand; it would have been running away, tail between legs, admitting defeat. It would have been what Jeremy wanted. But it would not have been the Italian way: there would have been no retreat without honour.

She had mixed with friends and relatives and she had watched Lorenzo out of the corner of her eye.

In retrospect, she could see that the explosion had been only a matter of time.

Jeremy had spent the afternoon showing her off, baiting his bitter rival. Little snide remarks scattered here and there, and then more often.

Isobel could remember gritting her teeth in frustrated anger at Jeremy's game-playing. He had always been fond of displaying his parents' wealth to Lorenzo.

Money. It had always been the one thing that had separated Lorenzo from the rest of them. His parents had come to England with very little, and although his father had held down a responsible job at one of the engineering companies, he had always had what had amounted, in comparison with the rest of them, a minuscule income. Lorenzo's school uniforms had been bought from the second-hand sales at the school, and text-books were never bought at all; they were borrowed from the library.

'Thinking about it, Isobel?' The smooth, cruel voice brought her back to the present, and she blinked and looked at him, disorientated.

'Thinking about what?' He had always had an amazing ability to read her mind, but she preferred to plead ignorance rather than to admit that he was spot on.

'Your glorious, happy wedding-day. So many people milling around, all the pillars of the little community, elaborately turned out for the affair of the year.'

'That's not fair!'

He continued as if she hadn't spoken. 'And of course you looked the part—you did your parents proud, Isobel, my dear.'

Isobel closed her eyes. She remembered the compliments. She had looked exquisite. She had been told that over and over again, and she had smiled prettily every single time. Her mouth had ached by the end of the evening.

'"Lucky Jeremy Baker." I could see the thought running through more than one envious male mind.' The dislike was thick in his voice and she kept her eyes lowered and her hands clenched in front of her. 'Lucky Jeremy Baker, netting the biggest fish in the sea. He paled next to you, but then everyone did, didn't they, Isobel?' he asked softly. 'Everyone except me.'

Her heartbeat quickened. She pictured them together, making love, his bronzed body wrapped against her flawless ivory one.

The thought flashed with startling clarity through her mind, and she shoved it back with a certain amount of disturbed confusion.

She remembered Jeremy. Slim, blond-haired, blue eyed, with that brand of good looks that were always charming in young children but in men were hardly ever sexy.

She had never found him particularly attractive. There was something in him that was vaguely unsettling, but they had always belonged to the same group of friends, drifting apart at one stage because of their age difference, but then drifting back again because in a town the size of theirs it was inevitable that they would. Their friends were all offspring of parents who, in their tiny community, knew each other very well.

'Why are we going over old ground?' she whispered helplessly, not daring to raise her eyes to meet his.

Breathing in his masculinity was making her head spin. Losing herself in those terrible, mesmeric eyes would only make the condition worse.

'Isn't that what old friends do?' he mocked harshly. 'Reminisce?'

'Old friends . . .?' The question hung in the air with a certain amount of pathetic sadness clinging to it, and he flung her aside abruptly, turning away to resume his position behind the desk. As if he owned it. As if he owned the entire office.

She hazarded a glance at him through lowered lashes. This situation was bizarre, ridiculous. If she had any sense at all, she would gather her wits about her, toss him a cool smile and walk out. Instead she listened to the silence, thick as lead, and sat back down in the chair.

Other unwanted memories of that wedding-day came back to her, relieved to be out at last from their exile in the furthest reaches of her mind—Abigail telling her with brutal frankness that she supposed congratulations were in order.

'Only if you really think so,' Isobel had replied, shoving the sleeves of the hateful wedding-dress up as far as they would go.

'You'll wreck your dress doing that.'

'Who cares?' she had answered, and had received a shrewd look in return.

'You should,' her friend had said. 'This should be neatly dry-cleaned and then carefully placed into storage somewhere for the line of little Jeremy Bakers you'll no doubt be producing over the next few years.'

'Never!'

Well, she thought now, at least that much had proved true. A child would have been the ultimate madness and she had never, not even once, been tempted, although all around her friends and acquaintances were having children and trying to persuade her that it was the next step.

'You've changed.' The observation, spoken without thinking, took her by surprise. She hadn't meant to say that. She had meant to inform him that she would be on her way now that he would no longer be buying her father's firm, because marriage as a condition was out of the question.

He sat back in the black swivel chair and looked at her with a shuttered expression.

'Yes, Isobel, I'm now wealthy and successful.'

'That's not what I meant.'

He shot her an angry look which would have driven her into silence if she had let it, but she was damned if she would be at the receiving end of all the blows.

'I'm not interested in hearing your thoughts on the matter,' he grated, tapping restlessly on the blotting-pad with his finger.

'Why not?' she flung at him bitterly. 'And besides, why should I care whether you're interested in hearing what I have to say or not? You patently don't give a damn about me!'

'Hurt, Isobel?' he threw back at her, and his eyes glittered like silver. 'Disappointed that I wasn't prepared to pick up the pieces of our relationship from where you ditched it on the roadside four years ago?'

'Of course not.'

'You over-estimate your charm. You might turn any number of heads here, but you forget that America is not entirely devoid of its share of lovely women.'

He was watching her closely, like a scientist observing a live specimen, waiting to see how it would react to various stimuli.

Isobel maintained her calm with effort.

'I do not "over-estimate" my charm, as you put it, nor am I aware of any amount of head-turning going on here, and I'm quite sure that America is bursting with lovely women—whatever that remark is supposed to mean.'

His lips tightened and she could tell he wasn't impressed with her retort. Did he really expect her to surrender in this war without a fight? Had he expected to waltz back here and make her dance to his tune without a murmur? She was sick to death of dancing to other people's tunes. She smiled guilelessly at him.

'I take it you've wined and dined your fair share of lovely women? Is that what you're trying to say to me?' She didn't like the thought of that and, more than that, she didn't like the thought that he could still provoke this level of wild jealousy inside her.

'What makes you think that I did the wining and dining?' he asked with a certain amount of mockery. 'Equality is rampant over there.'

That, she knew, was a lie. She couldn't see him allowing any woman to pay her way. It wasn't his style at all. With all her immense family wealth, he had never once allowed her to pay for a single meal. Instead they had eaten out at cheap bistros or else made do with bread and cheese on the bed. Followed by love. Her body warmed at the thought of that and she looked at him furtively, then glanced down at her entwined fingers.

No, Lorenzo Cicolla was Italian through and through. No amount of expensive American tailoring could ever change that.

She remembered how she had reacted on her wedding-day to his announcement that he would be leaving the country.

After the initial shock had worn off slightly, she had murmured to him in a low voice, 'You never told me that you were thinking of going to America.' Around them various voices were arguing, debating the pros and cons of starting life without any financial help, an argument initiated by the revelation of his trip abroad to play the options market.

'Would it have made the slightest difference?' he had asked cuttingly, and she had remained silent.

The silences between them were the things that she remembered most clearly about that torturous time, the things which she could not reveal, the words she could never say.

'I thought not,' he had said in an icy voice, and her eyes had pleaded with him for some understanding but had hit a blank wall of hostility. 'My post-grad results will be excellent but I don't think I'll return to this little hot-bed of intrigue to wait for them. No, I've already booked my flight.'

Then she had asked, in a dull voice, 'Where will you stay?'

'In a slum, I expect.' He had smiled a cool smile. 'As we both know, penthouse apartments are out of the question for someone who hasn't got parents rich enough to lend a convenient hand.'

Her face burned now as she thought back to her answer to that.

'I could give you——' she had begun and he had snarled savagely.

'Don't even say it. Charity is something I find repellent.'

Charity, she thought, looking at him, was clearly not an emotion he had assiduously cultivated in America. Oh, no. Charity couldn't be further from his mind in this demonic deal he wanted to cut.

'You'll be bored to tears within a month of living here,' she said, thinking prosaic thoughts so that the tingling in her blood could subside and return to its rightful place in a past which was no longer relevant.

'Oh, I think the element of novelty should keep me going for a while.'

She knew what he was referring to. The novelty would be her. When he tired, he would leave. They looked at each other, thinking the same thought—enemies on the same wavelength.

'In that case, you'll have to make do without the novelty of my father's company, because there is no way that your condition for buying the firm will be met.'

She stood and he said softly, 'Sit back down. I've already made it clear to you that you don't leave this office until I'm through.'

'And I've already made it clear to you that you don't run my life.'

'Hasn't Mr Clark told you what you can expect if I *don't* buy the company?' he said idly, clasping his hands behind his head and surveying her through narrowed eyes.

'He said that the company has great potential and a large client portfolio,' she replied, siphoning off most of what he had, in fact, told her.

'It's struggling to make ends meet. In less than a year its potential will be a nostalgic memory and its large client portfolio will be a thing of the past.'

'A year is a long time,' Isobel interjected mutinously. 'Anything can happen in a year.'

'For instance?' He appeared no more than mildly interested in her answer, which infuriated her more than if he had retaliated with some scathing, pithy observation.

'For instance,' she snapped, racking her brains to think of a few intelligent and probable for-instances, 'I could find someone to run the company on my behalf!'

'Who?'

'Well, if I had someone in mind, I wouldn't be here, would I?' she said heatedly. 'Humiliating myself.'

His eyebrows rose. 'Humiliating yourself?' he asked, as though the thought of her humiliation had not crossed his mind in any way, shape or form. 'Sure that's the emotion you had in mind?'

He stood up and strolled over to her, and she looked at his approaching figure with growing alarm.

'What are you talking about?' she asked, in such a breathless voice that she felt obliged to clear her throat and say as normally as she could, 'I don't know what you're talking about.'

He was close to her, staring down at her, and she looked up at him with impotent frustration.

Why couldn't he have stayed put? Why couldn't he have obliged and become a distant memory? Memories could be painful but they could also be dealt with. His presence here was altogether more intrusive and not one that she had ever bargained for.

Living with Jeremy had done wonders for her self-control. She had built a fortress around herself, a protective moat which no one could cross, and behind that moat she had concealed herself.

Now Lorenzo Cicolla had come back and already she was beginning to find cracks in her armour.

He raised his hand and ran one long finger along her cheek in a gesture so unexpected that for a second her heart seemed to stop beating.

'Ever since you laid eyes upon me, your colour's been a little on the hectic side,' he said softly, with a trace of cool mockery in his voice.

'Anger does that to a person,' she muttered as his finger trailed along her neck. 'Will you please remove your hand?'

'Why?'

'Because it makes me feel acutely uncomfortable.'

'Why does it?'

'Because,' she said, trying to sound controlled, 'I don't relish being touched by a man who hates me.'

'Are you quite sure, Isobel? Your mouth says one thing but your body is telling me something altogether different.'

He reached down without taking his eyes off hers, and she felt his hand cup the swell of her breast, neatly encased in its expensive grey wool suit.

There was nothing neat about her reaction, though. She had an instant of feeling that everything had plummeted out of control. Her breast seemed to enlarge, and her nipple hardened, longing for that touch to go further.

Her breath caught sharply in her throat and she pulled away.

'How dare you?' she said, choked and furious, with herself and with him. 'How dare you?' She was running the risk of spluttering now, so she fell into silence and made do with looking at him with icy hostility.

She had forgotten what a man's touch felt like. Her body had lapsed into a self-imposed celibacy and she had told herself that making love was something she didn't need. How wrong she had been. Lorenzo's brief caress, which stemmed from no more than a cruel need to prove his point, had aroused her to a pitch which she had never imagined possible.

She folded her arms around her, warding off any more potential invasion of her privacy, and glared at him.

'You were saying?' he prompted, as though the little interlude had not occurred.

Isobel looked at him and wondered dazedly what he was talking about now.

'About your grand ideas for saving your father's company?' he continued, walking across to the window and peering down with his back to her.

It was hardly reassuring talking to a back. She got the distinct impression that reassurance was the one thing he did not intend to extend to her, and he was making the point perfectly clear without uttering a word.

'I have no one specific in mind to run the company,' she said in a glacial voice, while he continued to lavish his attention on what was, she knew, hardly a spectacular view. 'But I'm sure it would be no problem finding someone.'

'From where?' he asked, not bothering to turn around. 'Off the street?'

'There are such things as employment agencies.'

He slowly turned around, reluctant, no doubt, she thought sourly, to abandon his fascination with the view of a half-empty pavement.

'What sort of person would you ask them to trot along to you?' he asked. He lounged indolently against the window-frame and appeared to find her thoughts on the matter vaguely amusing.

'Someone qualified,' she informed him.

'Qualified in what?'

'In triple by-pass surgery,' Isobel snapped, which appeared to amuse him still further. 'In running a company, of course.'

'Ah.' He paused, then asked with a frown, 'How do you know that he would be any good?'

'I'm not a moron. I would use my instinct.'

'Speaking as an ex-medical student? I'm impressed. And what would you do with the existing members of the board? Put them out to pasture? You know all of them personally. Can you really afford to make yourself unpopular in a town of this size?'

His logic infuriated her. 'I'd keep them on,' she snapped.

'And lose money even faster. What a shrewd business brain you're displaying here.'

'I'll take my chances. I'd rather do that than get myself involved in any sort of alliance with you.'

The cool amusement left his face as though it had never been there.

'You've become very self-righteous over the years,' he said with icy dislike. 'I don't recall such an attack of primness four years ago when you threw your lot in with Jeremy Baker. You never loved him but that certainly didn't stand in the way of progress, did it? How did you manage to justify that to yourself, Isobel? Did you grin and bear it and think of England? Was the union of two such illustrious families worth it?'

'You're hateful!'

'That's rich coming from you.'

'You can't buy me, Lorenzo.' Even as she said it she knew how ridiculous it sounded. To all intents and purposes, she had been bought four years ago. She tasted the bitter truth on her tongue and fought it back.

She remembered some of Jeremy's choice remarks at the wedding-reception.

'You might have had a lot going for you, Lorenzo,' he had said at one point, after he had consumed too much alcohol, and his tongue, already too loose, had loosened still further. The three of them had been sitting alone at the main table. She could still remember how embarrassing it had been. 'But,' he had continued in a slurred, resentful voice, 'money was the one thing that you never had. For God's sake, your mother used to work in some of our houses!' He had laughed then, as though he had made some particularly amusing observation, but neither of them had joined in.

'Money buys everything,' Lorenzo now said scathingly, 'and you are no exception.'

'Money can't buy happiness. It can't buy love. It can't buy respect. It can't buy health.'

Lorenzo looked away. 'How philosophical,' he commented sarcastically, and she sighed, weary with the whole damned thing.

'Please don't do this,' she said evenly. 'I know that you were upset when I married Jeremy...'

'Upset! You English! Yes, I was *upset*.'

'Not so upset that you didn't vanish to America without a backward glance; not so upset that you didn't cavort with God knows how many "lovely women"!'

'Did you expect me to keep in touch with you, Isobel? Write you pining letters so that you could wisely try and mend a broken heart from across the Atlantic?'

'You haven't got a heart.'

His face hardened. 'I'm a lucky man, in that case.' He paused, then asked in a voice that was edged with contempt, 'Was that what you wanted? To have me keep in touch even though you were married? Carry on being lovers while you and Jeremy played the perfect couple to one and all?'

'That's disgusting!' Colour rushed to her face.

'There are more disgusting things,' he said harshly, and she wished desperately that she could find the strength to walk away from this dark stranger who wanted to hold her life in his hands so that he could crumble it in his fist whenever he chose.

He was casting his mind back. She could see it. She knew what he was thinking. It was a memory that had haunted her for four years. The memory she had tried hardest to kill. But like all bad memories it had planted roots and refused to go.

'Don't tell me that you've forgotten that pretty little scene in your parents' garden four years ago?' His face was set in lines of bitter hatred.

'It's stupid delving back into the past,' she mumbled in a woolly attempt to avoid the unavoidable.

'I was in the garden. Jeremy followed me. He hadn't yet got his fill and I was actually beginning to regret my decision to stick out the damned thing when the most sensible thing would have been to decline his best man invitation and to face the fact that some challenges to one's honour had to be surrendered.'

'He had had too much to drink.' Her voice was a whisper.

'Always had been over-fond of the bottle, hadn't he, our dear Jeremy? He followed me into the garden and took up where he had left off.'

She remembered. She had been chatting to her mother while out of the corner of her eye she had noticed their departure from the marquee. She could recall thinking, Well, at least any argument wouldn't be overheard. She might not have wanted the wedding, but on the other hand she hadn't particularly wanted to see it degenerate into an all-out fight between the bridegroom and the best man.

As soon as she possibly could, she had followed them both. At first she hadn't seen them. It was a very large garden, landscaped, with quite a few trees and clumps of rhododendron. It had been designed with a view to being informal but arresting, and she had had to peer around a bit before she saw the two figures by one of the trees.

They had been arguing, that much was clear from the stance of their bodies. Jeremy had been gesticulating rather a lot, but Lorenzo's body had been rigidly still and, as she had approached she had seen that his expression was one of tightly controlled anger.

'Always money, wasn't it, Isobel?' Lorenzo asked tightly. 'The great insurmountable divide.'

'No.' The monosyllabic answer was a weak denial. It hadn't been money, not with her, never with her, but how could she explain that to him without revealing the secret which she was forced to clutch to herself?

He was pushing her into confronting things which she would be unable to defend, even now. She looked into his eyes and read the relentless fury there, still burning after all this time.

'No? You must have an extremely short memory, in that case.' His voice was cool and silky, but his expression wasn't. There was a tautness about his dark features that sent a shiver through her.

'Stop,' she said, and he gave a short laugh.

'If I recall, money was all that mattered to you, wasn't it?'

Isobel didn't answer. Her mind flew back to that scene in the garden when she had been called upon to defend Jeremy, to agree by her silence that money had mattered, that it had been the one thing which Lorenzo could never give her and the one thing that had severed their relationship.

'My darling wife,' Jeremy had said, with a smile of sly triumph, 'told me that you weren't good enough for her. She said that poverty was all right for a while, that it could be quite bohemian in a way, but that in the end it would be just too uncomfortable for her.'

And she had not been able to defend herself. Her hands had been tied.

Lorenzo had looked at her with bitter contempt, the same way that he was looking at her now, the same way that he had looked at her the minute he had set foot in

Mr Clark's office. He had forgotten nothing and he was not prepared to forgive. He would never be prepared to forgive. He would extract every ounce of blood from her and he would use whatever method came to hand to do it.

She felt the mounting despair of someone caught in a long, dark tunnel with no light at the end of it.

Jeremy's death should have brought her release, but instead she had jumped out of the frying-pan into the fire.

'Here's your big chance to set the record straight, Isobel. No Jeremy around now.' He gave her a long, leisurely, cool look. 'I'm waiting with bated breath for your version of what was said. I'm waiting for you to tell me that it was all a terrible mistake, an error of judgement on my part.'

'Why should I tell you anything?' she answered, and a look of savagery flashed across his face, quickly replaced by cold, bored mockery. 'You wouldn't believe a word I said anyway. You wouldn't want to. You came back here because, unexpectedly, circumstance has opened up an opportunity for you to make me suffer. I have no intention of throwing myself on your mercy. I'm not a fool.'

'You've always been a fool, Isobel Chandler,' he said in a voice that could have cut glass. 'You were a fool to become involved with me in the first place. I attracted you because I was from the wrong side of the tracks, and that sort of thing can hold quite a bit of appeal to a girl of your impeccable upbringing, can't it? But you made a grave mistake, my darling. You're right. Circumstance has thrown me a lifebelt, and I have every intention of using it.'

'I won't allow this,' she said, confused and frightened by the intent in his eyes. He had always been single-minded; he had always possessed the sort of personality that gauged a situation, assessed the outcome and then went for it. His ferocious drive had amused and bewitched her once because she had seen it through the eyes of a girl in love. Now she wasn't amused or bewitched. She was standing in its path, and all she could see was herself being rollercoastered into bits.

'I have nothing further to say to you,' she informed him. 'I won't sell my father's company to you, whatever you offer.'

'Oh, I shall have control of it, Isobel, just as I shall have control of you. There's no point fighting. It's only a matter of time.'

He walked across to the office door, opened it, and within minutes Mr Clark was hurrying in.

Isobel looked at him and should have felt a feeling of relief, but she didn't. All she felt was dread at the dark threat behind Lorenzo's words.

'All sorted out, I hope?' Mr Clark bustled to his desk, his eyes busily glancing at the two of them and apparently not registering anything amiss in the atmosphere.

'Not quite.' Lorenzo sat down on the chair opposite the desk and crossed his legs elegantly.

'Ah.' That obviously stumped Mr Clark. 'What appears to be the problem?'

'I won't sell.' Isobel spoke calmly but firmly. In the chair next to her she could feel Lorenzo. Some weird sixth sense seemed to register his presence so that every pore of her being was in a state of tense awareness. It was a feeling she hated because she had not felt vulnerable for a long time; she had learned to hide within herself, and to depend on that carefully cultivated talent for self-control.

'She'll sell,' Lorenzo said smoothly. 'There are just a few rough edges to work through. A few terms and conditions to be agreed upon.'

She didn't need to see his face to imagine the utter confidence written there. Mr Clark was clearly convinced. He looked relieved and settled back comfortably in his chair. Things would progress as normal. Never mind her objections. They were technicalities.

She badly wanted to protest but she didn't.

This was neither the time nor the place to indulge in a debate on the subject. But Lorenzo Cicolla was not going to have his way. If he wanted war, then she would fight.

CHAPTER FOUR

'How absolutely delightful for you, darling.' Mrs Chandler looked at her daughter with a smile, but Isobel refused to smile back. It was all of a week since she had set eyes on Lorenzo, and that week had been ample time in which to feed her growing panic at the prospect of his moving back to England to live.

He hated her. That had been evident in the cold, contemptuous slant of his eyes every time he had looked at her in Mr Clark's office, in the curl of his lips, in the well-chosen cruelty of his words. And now, four years on, he had the wherewithal to make her feel his hatred.

She looked at her mother, now frowning, and said as tactfully as she could, 'Mum, he's changed. He's not the man you used to know.'

'People don't change overnight, Isobel.'

'Four years is hardly what I would call overnight!' She stood up and began clearing away the dishes, and her mother began helping her. Isobel took this as a good sign. For the past few months she had been too lethargic, too wrapped up in her unhappiness to do anything, but recently, over the past couple of weeks, Isobel had noticed little changes in her mother.

'What I mean, darling, is that *fundamentally* people don't change. Oh, their fortunes may go up or down, their lifestyles may alter, but basically, they always remain the same.'

'Your theory falls down when it comes to Lorenzo Cicolla,' Isobel informed her, not wanting to prolong the conversation, but not quite knowing how to terminate it. 'He's become cold and ruthless. Why do you think that I have reservations about selling to him?' Start, she had thought, with the *reservations* ploy, so that when downright denial became inevitable her mother would find it easier to accept. As it was, it had taken quite some doing to convince her mother that selling immediately wouldn't have been the best option. After all, they both *knew* Lorenzo, didn't they? They both *knew* him for an honourable man who would see that everything was handled in a thoughtful and fair manner, didn't they?

They had cleared the table and Isobel turned on the tap, running the water until it was the right temperature, then filling the sink and piling the plates and cutlery in.

'Darling, I do think you're exaggerating a little.' Mrs Chandler picked up a tea-towel and began drying. 'You probably felt a little awkward with him because you used to go out with him.'

Now *that*, Isobel thought resentfully, was definitely not on the conversation agenda. So much water had flowed under the bridge since that time that whole landscapes had changed in the process.

'What are you planning to do tomorrow?' Isobel asked, adopting diversion tactics, and received a sly, amused glance from her mother.

'Of course,' Mrs Chandler said, 'I shall have to meet him. It's only polite, after all.'

'I have no idea where he is, and anyway why on earth do you have to meet him?' Isobel retorted, keeping her face steadfastly averted. 'It's hardly as though the deal has gone through. It's hardly as though he *owns* the company. We don't owe him a debt of gratitude.' Strong stuff, Isobel thought, biting back the urge to carry on for several hours in the same vein.

'Whatever went on between the two of you in Mr Clark's office?' her mother asked curiously.

'Nothing. Money and power's gone to his head, that's all,' Isobel muttered. 'There. Dishes done. Coffee?' She poured them both a cup and they retired to the sitting-room.

Outside, the autumn evening was drawing in and the light was deep and gold. It filtered through the trees in the garden and skirted across the well-maintained lawns. Isobel had arranged for two of the local lads to do the garden twice a week and, despite a few feeble protests, Mrs Chandler had been quite relieved.

'Darling, I know that you're handling this business, but any decisions must finally be taken with my agreement, mustn't they?' Mrs Chandler picked up the conversation as though there had been no lapse in between. 'It would seem very odd, don't you think? Having nothing to do with him when he is thinking of buying the company and, more to the point, when he is, after all, a family friend?'

'No.'

Isobel sprawled back in the chair and tried to look sleepy in the hope that it might deflect her mother's temporarily one-track thought processes. Lorenzo's return, she realised, had coincided with her mother's re-entry into day-to-day living, and it was providing her with a great deal of fodder with which to take her mind off her own personal worries.

'You're being difficult, Isobel.'

'No, I'm not,' Isobel said, and she heard the sulky petulance in her voice with irritated amusement. 'It's just,' she continued in a crisper tone, 'that I don't see the point of making a fuss over Lorenzo Cicolla just because he's decided to return to Deadsville, Yorkshire, as he no doubt sees us here, or even because he thinks he's going to buy Chandlers and have the opportunity to lord it over us. Why should we?'

'Because you were very fond of him at one stage, and of course, dear, I remember him quite clearly as a young boy, and I'd like to see how he is now!'

Isobel sighed in frustration and then shrugged.

'Well, I'm sure something can be arranged if he re-surfaces,' she added. 'Quite likely immediate lack of success in getting what he wants has put him off and he's taken himself elsewhere.' Never in a million years would she admit it, but, for the past week, she had found herself looking out for him, even though she hated herself for doing so.

'Perhaps you could check for me,' Mrs Chandler suggested, and Isobel gave her a horrified stare.

'Check?' she asked. 'Check? *Me*? After everything I've just said?'

'Yes,' her mother answered serenely. 'Would you object, darling? I do think it would be a nice gesture if we had him over to dinner. Just something light, of course. Apart from everything else, I'd like to discuss any hold-ups to the sale of the company. I'm convinced something can be worked out.'

'Dinner? Discussions? *Work things out*?' She sounded strangled and quickly swallowed some of the coffee.

'What else?' Mrs Chandler stood up. 'I think I shall retire now.' She moved towards Isobel and kissed her on the top of her head. 'It should be easy to trace him, though I'm sure he'll be in touch soon to resume discussions. Let me know just as soon as a day has been fixed. You and I can prepare something.' She smiled wistfully. 'Do you know, I shall never forget those wonderful parties your father and I used to throw. All the neighbours,' she sighed. 'I don't expect I shall ever do that again. But it will be nice seeing a different face, and

Lorenzo was always such a charmer.' She sighed again and Isobel followed her slow walk to the door before falling back into the chair with a little depressed groan.

Damn Lorenzo Cicolla. She would have been happy to put the past behind her; there were so many questions she had been dying to ask him, but he had made his hostility clear from the start, and if she had felt any warmth for him, it had been killed before it could take root.

She stood up, collected the empty cups and took them into the kitchen.

Of course, she had no choice but to ask him to dinner. Her mother already thought it peculiar that she had been so antagonistic in her reactions to him when to her, as to any outsider, he would appear an old friend.

She spent the following two days wondering whether she could convincingly develop temporary amnesia on the subject of Lorenzo Cicolla, whether she should make a token effort to find out where he was staying, perhaps a quick phone call to the least likely place for him to be, or whether she should simply make do with nothing under cover of reassuringly agreeing with whatever her mother suggested.

As it turned out she was spared having to do anything at all because she bumped into him quite by chance as she was cycling back from the surgery after work. Or rather he cornered her in his car, pulling up against the kerb so that she was hedged in and forced to dismount.

'I thought it was you,' he said coolly, stepping out of the Jaguar, and Isobel reluctantly stood facing him, her hands gripping the handlebars.

He was wearing dark trousers and a white shirt rolled to the elbows, even though there was quite a cool feel to the air.

'Lorenzo,' she said woodenly. 'What a surprise. I thought you might have changed your mind about coming back here now that you no longer have any reasons to remain.' Her heartbeat had unobligingly gone into overdrive and she tried to ignore that disastrous sensuality which he exuded without having to try.

'You didn't really think that,' he inserted with equal cool politeness. 'You knew that I'd be back.'

'How would I know that when you weren't around?'

'You mean that you've been looking out for me, Isobel? How flattering.'

Trust him, she thought sourly, to misconstrue an entirely innocuous remark. She looked at him with dislike and said, 'It's rather crowded here, and I'm late home, so if you don't mind...' That damned dinner invitation would just have to wait. She knew that her mother had a valid point, that decisions to do with the company had to be taken with her approval, but right now she felt unsettled and in no mood to prolong their conversation.

That wonderful sexual excitement which he used to induce in her all those years ago had now been replaced by feelings of muted panic and unease and a stupid stirring in her blood which, she told herself, irritated her more than anything else.

He didn't get back into his car. He remained staring at her, then he said, with a cursory glance around him, 'You're right, it is crowded here. Everyone leaving work.' He slammed shut the door and locked it.

'I won't keep you. My answer still stands.' She began to cycle off but he moved around the car with something approaching the speed of light and gripped the handlebars so that she was forced to stop.

'What do you think you're doing?' she asked furiously, looking up into those light, mesmerising eyes and feeling even more unsteady.

'So why don't we adjourn to the coffee-shop?'

'What for?' Her heart was racing but she continued to look straight at him.

'Now, now, is that any way for two old friends to treat one another?'

'The coffee-shop will be closed,' Isobel informed him bluntly, 'so I'm afraid we'll have to postpone the friendly chat for some other time.'

'In that case there must be a café or a wine bar within striking distance.'

'I have plans for this evening, Lorenzo,' she lied.

'What plans?'

'That's none of your business.'

'Come along. I want to talk to you.'

'I am not "coming along" anywhere. And, believe it or not, I have nothing to say to you. You made your position perfectly clear the last time we met! I was prepared to meet you in friendship and instead you chose warfare.'

'And were you upset, Isobel darling?' he drawled, and the colour shot into her face.

'I am too indifferent towards you to be upset by anything you say or do,' she replied quickly, and he gave her a slow, disbelieving smile.

'I'm cut to the quick,' he murmured.

She was, she discovered, feeling more flustered by the minute. 'What do you want, Lorenzo?' she asked in a low, hurried voice. 'There's nothing further to discuss about my father's company. You hate me and I understand that...'

His hand shot out to grip her arm. 'How very sympathetic of you.'

'These confrontations aren't going to get either of us anywhere.'

'Is that pub still open? The one old Wilkins used to run?' The snarl was no longer on his face. The coolness was back. The cat was once again toying with the mouse.

'Sam Wilkins died two years ago,' Isobel said. 'Not that I intend to stay here and run through life histories with you.'

The sarcasm was lost on him. He slipped his arm around her waist and before she could struggle had removed her bodily from the bicycle. Isobel sprang back from him, shaking from head to toe. The suddenness of the action had unnerved her, and the feel of his hands on her had been an electric shock to her system. It reminded her too dramatically of how she had felt in that office when he had touched her.

'Stop looking so wide-eyed, Isobel,' he said with a slight sneer. 'We both know that you're not sweet sixteen and never been kissed. We both know that you sold yourself to the highest bidder, so spare me the outraged expression.'

'Get lost, Lorenzo Cicolla,' she snapped, but keeping her voice down because she didn't need rumours spreading like wildfire through the town.

His mouth tightened. 'In a minute, one of these kind passers-by is going to step over and ask whether everything is all right. Isn't it easier just to come with me?'

'So that I can be insulted?'

'How,' he asked smoothly, 'can I possibly insult you when you claim to be so indifferent to me?'

She glared at him and he gave a bark of laughter, but he won, because when he turned away she found herself walking alongside him, her fingers wrapped so tightly around the handlebars that they hurt.

The pub, which was the very last building on the High Street, was fairly empty. The landlord, Sam Wilkins's son, whom she could remember as an overweight adolescent a few years older than she was, smiled at her, but his attention was on Lorenzo.

'Good to see you after all this time.' He nodded curtly, pouring them their drinks. 'Heard that you were going to be taking over Chandlers. News round here spreads faster on the grapevine than on a radio.' He placed their drinks in front of them. He was tall, rather florid in the face, and possessed a forthright tongue that had no respect for tact or diplomacy. 'Plan on staying long?'

'Long enough,' Lorenzo said, his eyes hooded.

Long enough, Isobel would have liked to add, to make my life a living hell. She took her drink and asked after Tom's wife and children.

'Town could do with some fresh blood,' Tom said, having confirmed the status of his wife and children and refusing to have his attention distracted by domestic chit-chat. He eyed both of them. 'And of course, with Jeremy gone...'

'Leave it alone, Tom!' Isobel said warningly, but Lorenzo laughed, with real amusement on his face.

'With Jeremy gone, what do you suggest, Tom?' he asked lazily, and Tom shrugged with a sheepish expression.

'Women aren't meant to be alone,' he stated, to which Isobel replied tartly,

'How very twentieth-century and forward-thinking of you, Tom.' Actually she was beginning to feel rather embarrassed, especially since she could feel Lorenzo's eyes on her.

They walked across to one of the circular oak tables by the fireside, and Isobel said crossly, 'Tom Wilkins should watch what he says. There's such a thing as an excess of honesty.' She sat down, crossed her legs and gave him a 'well, now that you've dragged me here, what do you want to talk to me about?' expression.

Lorenzo settled back in his chair, raised his glass to his lips and surveyed her over the rim.

'Makes a refreshing change from the hypocrisy I've encountered over the past four years out there in the concrete jungle.'

'You would soon get sick of it, were you to remain,' Isobel said coolly, and he raised his eyebrows.

'Is that wishful thinking on your part, or have you taken up amateur psychology in your spare time?'

'Hilarious,' she said, watching him. 'Now, what exactly would you like to talk about?' She looked at her watch meaningfully, which appeared to have the opposite effect of making him prolong his silence, while he contemplated her with something bordering on insolence.

'Actually, I thought you might be interested in what I had planned for your father's company.'

'You won't be taking over my father's company.'

'Nothing stands in my way when I've made up my mind. Another drink?' he asked, and she shook her head, furious at his arrogance.

'Some re-organisation,' he continued, as though she had not uttered a word. 'Do you know much about your father's business?'

'I told you, you won't be——'

'I will be taking over Chandlers, Isobel,' he grated, leaning forward, 'and I will be taking it over on my terms. Now, answer me: do you know anything about your father's company?'

'No,' she said tightly, deciding to humour him rather than sit through his relentlessness.

'Nothing at all?'

'No,' she snapped. 'Not that this line of conversation is relevant.'

'Good God, Isobel, what on earth have you been doing with yourself for four years?'

'I don't see what that has to do with anything!' she retorted hotly, flushing. He made her life seem so *trivial*. 'I work at the local surgery and it's a pretty full-time job. I hardly saw the need to take up a second career looking over my father's shoulder! Anyway, this is ridiculous. You might think that you can do what you want, that I'll give in to your bizarre conditions, but you're wrong!'

'I intend to streamline the whole operation. It's a bit like an octopus at the moment, with tentacles stretching here, there and everywhere, and very few of them reaping much by way of profit.'

'Those tentacles provide jobs,' Isobel hissed, temporarily side-tracked, and he looked at her with a hooded expression.

'I'll bear that in mind when I decide to make it a registered charity,' he said. 'Until then, the business has to shrink.'

'And to hell with the livelihoods that will be swept down the drain?' This seemed as good an area as any for letting off steam. Isobel took a deep breath. 'Some of the people there have worked in my father's company from the year dot. What do you intend to do with them when your great streamlining project gets under way? Throw them a few rueful platitudes about recession and pat them on the head?'

She expected him to get angry with her—in fact, if she was honest with herself, she quite wanted it because she dearly would have liked to release some of that pent-up, confused, alarming feeling that swept through her every time she saw him in a good raging argument. But he stared at her, then said in a low voice, 'So you do recognise that I plan on coming back here?'

'No.' She spoke sharply, reddening when she realised that she had been persuaded into an argument which had weakened her position.

'I lied when I said that I could resist you.' It was a statement of fact and there was no tenderness on his face when he spoke. 'You're as exquisite as you always were and I still want you.'

A dark excitement coursed through her and she looked away, alarmed.

His voice was husky, sexy. It made her senses spin and she had to force herself to say in a final tone, 'You can't expect me to sign myself over to you. I already...' She stopped, confused, and he moved forward, reaching out to hold her chin, to force her face to his.

'Made that mistake? Is that it, Isobel? Dammit, talk to me, woman!'

'There's nothing to discuss.'

'You betrayed me and I want to know why.'

His intensity unsteadied her and she made a heroic effort to regain her composure.

'Why won't you just let me be? Have my father's company. I'll sell it to you, but leave me alone.'

'Never,' he bit out, releasing her in an angry gesture.

There was a tense silence and she seemed to hear the workings of her body, the anxious, desperate beating of her heart, the mad flow of blood through her veins, the heavy thud of her pulse.

'Your plans for the company... What would you do with the people you laid off?'

'I'll allow you to change the subject for now,' he rasped, 'but only for now.'

It no longer mattered that he was going to tell her about plans which would never materialise. She would have welcomed any change of conversation. She would have gladly encouraged him to hold forth on metaphysics and its place in the kitchen if it had meant not having to withstand that terrible assault on her senses.

Besides, she told herself practically, she might gain an idea or two from what he had to say. Who knew, his suggestions might serve her well if it came to having to work things out for herself. *When*, she amended to herself, *when* it came to having to work things out for herself. She felt better now she could reason that one out, and she smiled encouragingly.

'I have an excellent redundancy package worked out, which will amount to early retirement for some of the older members of staff, all of whom will eagerly accept.'

'How do you know that?'

'Experience,' he answered with utter assurance. 'It's a misconception that most people want to devote as much of their lives as they can to working in an office. The majority would quite happily take early retirement and relax on the proceeds.'

Yes, she thought, that made sense.

'And who would you volunteer for early retirement? Hypothetically speaking, of course.'

Lorenzo was watching her through narrowed eyes and she wondered whether he was trying to gauge her sudden interest in a topic which she had only minutes before proclaimed to be a waste of her vocal cords. She hoped desperately that he would find nothing revealing on her face. Living with Jeremy had done a great deal to sharpen her powers of concealment. He had always enjoyed the hold that he had over her, and she had learned very early on that the more sensitive she appeared, the more he relished it, so in the end she had learned to disguise her emotions under a wall of blankness. Like all things, it had gradually become a second skin. Time could work wonders.

'Greg Thompson, Vic Richards, old McGraw—all of whom are doing the company no good at all. They lack the drive that they no doubt had in their younger days.' He paused. 'Of course, there would have to be some reshuffling, but strings would be pulled to help those men who suddenly find themselves out of work to pick up the pieces and carry on.'

'Greg Thompson,' Isobel murmured. 'Vic Richards, Ronnie McGraw.' Shame, she thought, that she didn't have a notebook.

'Any more questions?' he asked, raising his eyebrows. 'Sure you can remember the helpful hints?'

'Helpful hints?'

'You won't get the chance, Isobel, so forget it. No one touches that company but me. I'll make sure of that.' He smiled coolly and she wondered what it would feel like to tip the remainder of her drink over his head.

'I told you. You can have the company.'

'You're part of the deal.'

'Why?' she asked with a feeling of dreadful apprehension. 'Why marriage?'

'Because running your father's company isn't going to be a hobby for me. Of course, I have other businesses, some in America, and that will involve travel, but I also have men who can run them efficiently in my absence. No, I plan on settling down here and this is the sort of town where respectability is essential.' He looked at her through hooded eyes. 'Would you have agreed to be my woman on the side?'

Colour crawled into her face. 'Of course not.'

'I want you, Isobel, and I intend to have you. Marriage is a bonus for you.'

'And fidelity?' she asked bitterly. 'Love?'

'Since when has the absence of love held you back?' he asked softly.

She stared at him, dry-mouthed. It shocked her that he was prepared to go to such lengths to wreak his revenge. He didn't love her but he would marry her because he knew that marrying her was the one thing she wanted least.

Simply owning her father's firm would not be enough.

'And fidelity?' she asked, skirting round his question, which she could not answer without tying herself up in knots.

'What about it?'

'I see.' She did too. She saw that fidelity would mean absolutely nothing to him. 'You would feel free to indulge yourself whenever you wanted,' she observed bitterly.

'You see that, do you?'

The question hung in the air, tantalisingly asking for a response.

'I must go.' She stood up, half expecting him to prolong the conversation, relieved when he stood up as well.

'What's it like working with Adams?' he asked casually as they moved towards the door, and she threw him a surprised look.

'You told me that you worked at the surgery. There's only one.'

'Oh, yes.'

'Not that it mattered. I had you checked out before I came back anyway.'

'You had me what?'

She stopped by the door and stared at him in angry astonishment.

'Checked out,' he repeated calmly, as if they were discussing nothing more important than the weather. 'I thought that I might as well find out about you. I knew where you worked and for whom.'

'You had a detective trailing me?'

'Tom Wilkins will begin to get very interested if he sees us engaged in earnest conversation here.'

'Some seedy man in an overcoat, peering through binoculars?' she asked, aghast.

'Hardly. I asked Clark to find out about the family background, about you.'

'On what pretext?' The simmering phase was fast reaching a rolling boil. He pulled open the door and shoved her out and she turned on him angrily. 'That's the most despicable thing I've ever heard in my life!'

'You must have led a very sheltered life these past four years, in that case,' he said, unmoved.

'You had no right!'

'I was planning to spend quite some money buying your father's firm. I felt I had the right. Besides, I was curious.'

'You were curious. Well, that makes it all right then, doesn't it?'

They were walking along slowly and she made sure that she kept a very safe distance from him.

'Adams isn't married, is he?' Lorenzo asked in a casual voice.

'No.'

'What's he like? I remember him as looking like a giraffe. All limbs.'

'He's grown into a very attractive young man,' Isobel said stiffly. 'Not that it's any of your business.'

'Everything that has to do with you is my business.' He wasn't looking at her as he said that. He was staring straight ahead. Isobel glanced at him, at the hard profile, the lean, muscular body with its peculiarly graceful stride.

Abigail had once told her that she thought Lorenzo was remarkable, the sexiest man she had ever laid eyes on.

'He could go far in my line of business,' she had commented. 'He would make an imposing actor. He has the presence. He doesn't even need to open his mouth.'

Why hadn't he stayed put? Isobel wondered. Why hadn't he had the good manners to stay a memory, lurking at the back of her mind? Why did he have to bring his imposing presence back into her life? She had never recovered from him, but at least recovery would have been possible in the end if she was denied proximity.

Her only chance rested in his departing once again for distant shores.

She would never marry him; she would never give him his opportunity to wreak revenge, and perhaps, once he saw that, he would give up any attempt to persuade her.

'Cosy for you,' he said softly, next to her, 'working with a single, attractive man.'

'Yes.' Isobel turned to face him. 'We have a very good relationship.' She could have inserted 'working', but then why should she?

'And how did Jeremy feel about that?'

'Is this a question and answer session?' she asked politely as they reached her bike, and she grabbed hold of it and began walking along the pavement. 'Anyway, I'm surprised you didn't get your spy to fill you in on all these details. Lapse of yours.' She wished that he would vanish into thin air.

'Were you having an affair with him?' He reached out and gripped one of the handlebars.

'You can take it however you like,' she answered, and his mouth hardened.

'So you had an open marriage. I don't suppose I should be too surprised at that. Was Jeremy that nondescript in bed or did you feel that, once you had established your status quo, there was no need to pretend to feel anything for him? Or were you sleeping with both men at the same time, Isobel? If I recall, you always were a passionate little thing.'

Isobel's hands tightened on the handlebars until her fingers were white. She would have slapped him if she could, but little towns were not places for public fights, and she knew that he was deliberately playing with her anyway.

'I really must be going, Lorenzo,' she said, without looking at him, and his hand slid up to grip her arm.

'Not until you've answered my questions.'

Her response to that was to yank at her bike, and he let her, walking alongside her until they approached his car, at which point he held on to the bike and said, with the same semblance of politeness which didn't fool her for a minute, 'I'll drive you to your house.'

Isobel looked at him. In the gathering gloom of nightfall his face was all shadows and angles. A hard, powerful face, the face of a man who seldom, if ever, yielded to resistance.

'I want to meet your mother,' he said, his mouth twisting. In the darkness the grey eyes glittered with casual menace. 'After all, it won't be long before I shall know her very well indeed, will it, Isobel?'

CHAPTER FIVE

THEY drove the short distance to the house in silence. She could remember how much they had talked, years ago, planned, laughed, when any silences between them were filled with warmth. This silence was heavy with foreboding.

As soon as the car pulled up outside the house Isobel shot out, followed lazily by Lorenzo.

In a stroke of monumentally bad luck, as far as Isobel was concerned, her mother was at the door as it was pushed open.

She saw Lorenzo, and Isobel watched with a sinking heart the expression of warm delight on her mother's face, the exchange of greetings.

'How wonderful to see you, Lorenzo.'

Oh, God, Isobel thought. This had the makings of more than a five-minute chat on the doorstep.

'I suppose my daughter has arranged the dinner date with you? Naughty of her not to have phoned and warned me.' Her mother gave one of her throaty, relaxed laughs.

'No, as a matter of fact, she hasn't.'

'I forgot,' Isobel said. She stepped into the hall, blocking the entrance with her body, and said coolly, 'You must drop round some time for a meal, Lorenzo. Though I'm sure you'll be far too busy to accept in a hurry.'

'I should love to come round for dinner,' he replied, looking at her tight-lipped face with amusement.

'Why not now?' Mrs Chandler peered over Isobel's shoulder. 'There's a casserole in the oven—nothing terribly fancy, I'm afraid—and some vegetables from the garden.'

'I can't think of anything nicer,' he said with an infuriating smile, and he stepped past Isobel into the hall.

Her mother was right. Lorenzo Cicolla had great charm, an abundance of it. Hatred for her, she thought, had hidden it, but it was in full force now, and bowling her mother over by the second.

Both her parents had been very fond of him. She was tempted to point out the ruthlessness, the arrogance, the obliterating single-mindedness which rubbed shoulders with the dark, persuasive smile and the easy, sophisticated banter, but she held her tongue. Meeting her mother was a waste of time. He would discover that in due course.

They went to the sitting-room, with Isobel trailing behind them, listening to the warm exchange of two people who frankly liked each other and wishing that she could think up a suitable ailment that would spare her from what threatened to be a very uncomfortable evening ahead.

'Now,' Mrs Chandler said, after she had poured them all a drink, 'shall we get the uncomfortable part of this evening out of the way?'

Lorenzo raised his eyebrows in a question and Isobel felt her spirits sink a little lower. She swallowed her glass of wine in record time, helped herself to another to steady her nerves, and sat back.

'Sounds ominous,' Lorenzo drawled.

'I was absolutely delighted when Isobel told me the prospective buyer of David's company,' Mrs Chandler began, looking suitably delighted. 'It came as a great shock when Mr Clark told us that we would have to sell

Chandlers. You see, it was David's great love building
that company. I dreaded the thought of a stranger
coming along, maybe taking it to pieces. Someone with
no history in the community, commuting from another
town, seeing the firm as something to make a profit.'

Lorenzo nodded. Isobel eyed him sceptically from
under her lashes and wondered how much of that sympathetic air was real and how much feigned.

'I understand,' he murmured.

'Do you?' Isobel shot him an innocent look of raised
eyebrows and curved lips. 'Then I take it you approached every company you took over as a sympathetic
friend and not as an investor wanting to see his in-
vestment make money?'

Lorenzo frowned at her. 'I have always been fair in
my take-overs.'

'Oh, how reassuring,' she murmured with a sweet
smile.

'I told Isobel,' Mrs Chandler said hurriedly, giving
her daughter a reproving, sidelong look, 'that I couldn't
possibly foresee what the hitches might be. Perhaps you
feel the company, on closer inspection, is not worth what
you're prepared to pay? You can be quite honest with
us, Lorenzo. After all, we go back a long way.'

'Businessmen are never honest, Mum,' Isobel said.
'They're diplomatic. Like politicians and salesmen.'

'Your father was honest.'

Isobel looked away at that. She thought of Jeremy,
she thought of her marriage, she thought of sacrifices
made before she was even old enough to enjoy life to
the fullest.

'The price has nothing to do with it, Mrs Chandler,'
Lorenzo said abruptly into the silence. He leaned
forward, deposited his glass on the table in front of him
and relaxed back on the sofa. 'You say that you want

honesty, so I'll be blunt. This deal would have been wrapped up over a week ago, but I felt that I lacked the necessary co-operation from your daughter.'

'Isobel?'

Lorenzo glanced across to where Isobel was trying to conceal an expression of stony anger, and continued in an unhurried voice, 'I feel that in a town of this size it's imperative that I have every backing from the family members of the firm. Perhaps if I had been an outsider it would have mattered less, but everyone knows that Isobel and I know one another, and most people know that we were...involved at one point.'

'What does that have to do with it?' Isobel asked sharply, feeling her colour mount.

'Quite a bit. You see, if I take over Chandlers without the backing of your daughter, Mrs Chandler, it won't be long before tongues begin to wag. People will begin to wonder whether it was perhaps a hostile take-over, whether you had been forced to sell against your will. It would only be a short step before they began to have suspicions about me as a person. After all, Chandler has been a name in this town for as long as I can remember. Business would suffer because it would be impossible to operate successfully here with hostility in the air.'

'Don't you think you're exaggerating a little?' Isobel asked, recognising a trap and wriggling to squirm out of it.

He shook his head. 'In a big city you're anonymous. In a town like this you're not. There's a constant process of symbiosis at work. You think what would happen if Tom Wilkins sold his pub to someone who wasn't accepted. How long would it be before the pub began having trouble attracting customers? How long would it be before it was forced to close down completely?'

Mrs Chandler was nodding in slow agreement.

'I am perfectly willing to sell Father's company to him,' Isobel muttered, feeling guilty and then angry that she should when she had absolutely nothing to feel guilty about.

Was it her fault that he had laid down conditions which were impossible to meet? Was it her fault that he had returned with only one thing on his mind: revenge?

'You haven't been very enthusiastic though, darling, have you?' Mrs Chandler asked with gentle reproof, which made Isobel redden even more.

'Not enthusiastic at all,' Lorenzo murmured, in a disappointed voice, sliding his eyes across to her and only just managing to contain his amusement.

'Darling.' Mrs Chandler stood up and her voice was very firm. 'I hope you'll think very carefully about this; I hope you will do everything in your power to convince Lorenzo that he has your full backing. I shall go and see to the food and let you two discuss it between yourselves.'

'You...! You...! Words fail me, Lorenzo Cicolla!' she said as soon as the door closed behind her mother.

He smiled.

'Your mother *did* say that she wanted honesty.'

Isobel helped herself to another glass of wine, because her nerves needed further bracing, and tried to formulate a suitably scathing reply to that.

'You have to admit that what I said made sense,' Lorenzo carried on, before she could think of her scathing reply.

'I have to admit nothing of the sort!'

'Your mother agrees with me.'

'You talked your way around her,' Isobel muttered darkly. 'That lecturer of yours was right. You should have studied law. You have a mind devious enough.'

'Is that a compliment?' He looked perfectly relaxed, his mouth curved into an amused smile.

'No, but I'm sure you'll take it as one. How could you turn my mother against me?'

'I wasn't doing anything of the sort. I was simply pointing out that I needed your co-operation if this venture was to succeed the way I'd like it to.'

'Your idea of co-operation and my mother's idea of co-operation aren't exactly the same though, are they?' Isobel asked with sarcasm. 'What do you think she would say if I told her the truth? That what you had in mind wasn't along the lines of the occasional invitation to dinner and cheery greetings on the street, but a ring on my finger.'

'Who knows? She might be thrilled.'

'And if I told her that the only reason you wanted my so-called co-operation was for motives that had nothing to do with the company?'

'She probably wouldn't believe you.'

Their eyes met and Isobel felt her head spin. Too much wine. She hardly ever drank. She should have fortified her nerves with mineral water or orange juice.

She half closed her eyes and said, 'I feel giddy.'

'My poor darling,' he murmured, with a low, sexy laugh. 'Is that because you're overwhelmed at the re-alisation that you're going to marry me, like it or not, or because you've had too much to drink?'

'I haven't had too much to drink.'

'Three glasses.'

'I hate people who count how much other people have had to drink. And I'm not going to marry you.' She should be feeling angry, *furious*, in fact, but she really did feel light-headed, and somehow she couldn't summon up the energy for an argument.

When her mother returned and announced that dinner would be ready shortly, Isobel stood up, hoped that she would be able to walk a straight line across the room, and announced that she needed to go and change.

Under a stream of lukewarm water she tried to get her muddled thoughts into some kind of coherent order, and in the end abandoned the unequal struggle.

Lorenzo, who from of old could run rings round most people, had succeeded very thoroughly in running rings around her.

She wasn't going to give in, she knew that, but she felt too relaxed to think about how she was going to stop him without incurring her mother's disapproval.

When she emerged fifteen minutes later, in a pair of jeans and a jade-green jumper, she could hear her mother's laughter and Lorenzo's low, deep voice wafting from the sitting-room.

They both looked around as she walked in, and her mother, still smiling, said, 'No more shop talk tonight. Lorenzo's been telling me all about America. I've always wanted to visit there.'

'No, you haven't,' Isobel said, wondering whether she dared indulge in one last glass of wine—after all, the evening was hardly over—and deciding that she would. She felt much better after her shower. Not so languorous and floaty. 'You and Dad hated having holidays outside England. The few times you went to Europe you always came back looking exhausted.'

'True,' Mrs Chandler conceded with grace. 'But Lorenzo makes it sound terribly exciting.'

Lorenzo, Isobel wanted to point out, could make sitting in a room and watching paint dry sound terribly exciting.

She frowned. Of course that was a long time ago, before she discovered that she hated him. Or was it, she thought confusedly, and if it wasn't, then what did that mean?

'Did you know that he now owns several companies, darling?' her mother asked.

'Really?' Isobel tried to invest her voice with interest. 'Staggering. I'm deeply impressed.'

'It must have been terribly hard work,' Mrs Chandler said thoughtfully, turning her attention back to Lorenzo. 'I have heard that America is a very competitive place. Is it?'

'Highly.' He had helped himself to another glass of wine and he took a mouthful of it. 'For the first year I was there, I think I must have had two hours' sleep every night. I was working crazy hours. Not that I minded.' He laughed and Mrs Chandler laughed with him. When he decided to be charming, Isobel thought, there were very few people who could resist him, least of all members of the opposite sex.

'I was living in such a hell-hole,' he continued, 'that the office was palatial in comparison.'

'How awful for you,' Mrs Chandler said, looking at her daughter for some contribution to the conversation.

Isobel murmured obligingly, 'How horrendous. However did you cope?' She had worked it all out. If she were seen to be co-operating with him, at least in front of her mother, then, when the deal fell through, well, no blame could be laid on her doorstep, could it?'

Lorenzo was looking at her, his eyes narrowed and serious. 'I coped, Isobel, with thoughts of returning here in due course. I had gone to America to find success, and success was precisely what I intended to bring back here with me.'

'Very single-minded.' Her mother approved, apparently. She had married a man who had been ambitious as well. It was an ethos which she could understand. 'I

do so hope that you'll buy David's company.' Her eyes
lost some of their unreserved sparkle. 'I know it will be
in safe hands with you.' She turned to Isobel. 'You do
see, don't you, darling?'

'If you want me to,' Isobel muttered, which met with
a disapproving frown from her mother, and she quickly
amended her remark, adding, 'I'm sure Lorenzo would
make sure that it was firing on all cylinders in no time
at all.' *Be seen to co-operate*, she thought.

Her mother was nodding. 'David was worried about
it for quite some time before he died,' she said, which
made Isobel look at her in surprise. Her father had been
worried about the company? He had never let on!

'Why?' Lorenzo asked, and Isobel could see his ears
pricking up.

Mrs Chandler shrugged sadly. 'He knew that there
were loopholes in the management, but he was desperately against firing old friends, and of course quite a few
of the hierarchy in the company *were* old friends.' She
glanced at Lorenzo. 'You know what it's like here. We
all know one another.'

'A dangerous situation.'

'It can be, but also a comforting one. David spent so
much time trying to work out a solution. The only other
time I have ever known him to be worried to that extent
was years ago. He never told me what was wrong and
eventually, whatever it was, he sorted it out.' She stood
up. 'Well, so much for memory lane. I shall go and see
to that casserole. I'll call you when everything's ready.'

Which, of course, was Isobel's cue to jump up and
offer to do it instead, but her mother shook her head
and murmured, 'No, darling, you stay here and entertain Lorenzo. You haven't seen each other for such a
long time.' She looked at him with affection and Isobel

felt very much like telling her that she would do better to expend her affection on a swarm of killer bees.

'And remember, you two, no shop talk!'

As soon as Mrs Chandler had left the room, Lorenzo looked at Isobel, his eyes veiled.

'Still feeling giddy?' he asked. He sounded amused and she scowled at him.

'Not in the slightest,' she said airily.

'You soon will if you finish that glass of wine. Four was always your limit.'

Isobel blushed and finished the glass of wine. 'I'm surprised you remember that,' she remarked. 'With only two hours' sleep every night, for years on end, you'd think that your powers of recall might have dulled a bit.'

He laughed, and it was the laugh she had known years ago, that wicked, amused laugh that made her bones go funny. Or was it her imagination?

'Don't think that you're going to get your way just because I'm not arguing with you,' she rushed in, uncomfortably aware that the room was too hot, or too small, or too *something*, because she was feeling awfully conscious of his presence there on the sofa, semi-sprawled, his trousers contouring his muscular legs in a way that she found quite fascinating.

'Perish the thought.'

'You're enjoying this, aren't you?' Isobel asked, with less bitterness than she might have normally. 'You're enjoying watching my discomfort.'

'I have always enjoyed watching you, Isobel,' he said ambiguously, which made her go red. She stood up agitatedly and began pacing through the room, her body as tense as a coiled spring because she knew that his eyes were on her, following her.

'Oh, for goodness' sake, stop prowling,' he ordered, and she gave him a wry look.

'You've become very fond of giving commands, Lorenzo,' she said silkily, pausing next to his chair to look down at him.

With a swift gesture his fingers circled her wrist, and he pulled her down on to the arm of the chair. Only some instinctive sense of balance saved her from falling on to his lap, but the suddenness of the action winded her and she looked at him in angry embarrassment.

'That's better,' he said comfortably, still gripping her so that she had no option but to remain where she was or else initiate a struggle which she knew she would lose. He was a strong man. Right now he was pinning her down with ease, as effortlessly as a tiger pinning a mouse under its paw.

'You may think that the only reason I'm here is because I get some sort of vicarious thrill in putting your nose out of joint, but as a matter of fact I'm here because I wanted to see your mother, believe it or not. It's been a long time.' His voice was deep and velvety, and altogether hypnotising. Isobel looked at the dark, chiselled contours of his face and tried very hard not to betray her confused awareness of him.

'How is her illness?' he asked quietly, and she lowered her eyes.

'She copes with it. She always has.'

'She's always been a strong woman.'

'That's what Richard says.'

His eyes sharpened at that, as did his grip on her wrist.

'Ah. Dr Adams. We hadn't finished our little discussion on him, had we? Does he say that during working hours or out of them? Were you fooling around with the single, attractive Dr Adams? You haven't answered me that.'

'We're friends,' she informed him. Was he jealous? Her heart gave a swoop of pleasure at the thought of that, but the pleasure didn't last long. If he was jealous, it had nothing to do with emotional reasons. If he was jealous it would be because a man in her life would detract from her vulnerability and he wanted her vulnerable, he wanted her in a position where he could hurt her the way she had hurt him four years ago.

No amount of wine should relax her into forgetting that, she thought to herself.

Besides, she decided, why should it matter what he feels for me? She looked at that dark, handsome face and, somewhere at the back of her mind, an answer to that began to take shape. She shoved it aside quickly, though.

'She took Dad's death very badly,' Isobel heard herself saying in a hurried, nervous voice. 'They had been together for such a long time, I suppose, and, of course, she was always very dependent on him. He took care of everything. She had no idea how to manage the most basic of her finances.'

Was he listening to her? He was staring at her but he didn't appear to be taking in a word she was saying. She began to feel more addled.

'Can I have permission to return to my chair now?' she asked, clearing her throat.

His voice, when he answered was husky. 'No. I rather like you here.'

'And how is your mother?' Isobel stammered, clearing her throat again. She sounded breathless and a little choked. Would he believe her if she said that she had been suffering from a sore throat? Would he let her go if she told him that she was in dire need of a couple of throat lozenges? Perhaps she could mention her giddiness again, although right now she felt too rigidly tense to be giddy.

'Fine. Looking forward to the possibility of moving back here.' He idly crossed his legs and relaxed back in the chair. 'She's in Italy at the moment. She'll probably be there for a couple of months, until things are more settled here with me.' He absentmindedly began stroking the inside of her wrist with his thumb and her body began feeling feverish. 'Tell me what's been happening around here for the past four years,' he murmured softly, coaxingly. 'In a calm, non-argumentative fashion, because you're supposed to be co-operating with me, aren't you?'

'It would take too long.' She fidgeted on the arm of the chair. 'Besides, I'm very uncomfortable in this position.'

'Are you?' he asked with a wicked smile, then he pulled her down so that she tumbled in an undignified heap on to his lap, and she began to struggle uselessly.

'What the hell do you think you're up to?' she said, out of breath. He had one arm around her neck, and the other resting on her thighs. She wriggled again, and the arm moved from her thighs to her chest, so that his hand was spread just beneath her breastbone. She wasn't wearing a bra, and under her jumper she could feel her breasts grow heavy and painful, she could feel her nipples hard, aching, erect with excited longing.

'My mother,' she said, enunciating as carefully as she could, 'will have a heart attack if she walks into this room and finds us like this.' She was so close to him that she could see the little flecks of deeper grey in his irises, the fine lines around his eyes. She knew that if she wasn't careful his nearness would go to her head like incense, and—and what? she wondered with an inward shudder.

'It might force us to tell her that I intend to be her son-in-law. Besides, she's safely ensconced in the kitchen, taking care of dinner,' he murmured.

'There's just so much time someone can spend on preparing vegetables and setting a kitchen table,' Isobel said, ignoring his suggestion, even though it stirred something in her, something treacherous, a reluctant fire waiting to be rekindled. Keep it calm, she told herself shakily, pretend that his hand isn't inches away from your breast, that his mouth isn't inches away from yours, and you'll be all right.

Lorenzo ignored that. 'When you married him,' he muttered, 'I spent so long going quietly mad at the thought that you would be making love to him.' His hand moved to cup her breast and he groaned slightly as though surprised and dismayed by an involuntary reflex action over which he had no control.

Isobel gasped. Her breathing was forced and erratic and she had a terrible feeling that if she closed her eyes she would never resurface back to reality. She kept her eyes wide open and reminded herself that this was a man who felt nothing for her but fury and dislike. The fact that her body was longing to respond to his touch was a temporary heat against which she knew she had to fight because if she gave in to him, even momentarily, she would never be able to live with herself again. It was the wine. She should never have had that fourth glass. He had been right.

'Let me go,' she said, in as normal a voice as she could muster. 'I don't want to talk about him or about my marriage. I don't want you to touch me.'

'Don't you?' he whispered. 'You want me as much as I want you.'

'No.' She moved but it was a weak gesture. Her limbs felt like lead. She wanted to move, to run away, but her body was no longer functioning. It had decided to stay put.

He looked at her, and his finger moved to toy with her nipple until she wanted to scream out in frustrated longing. She clenched her fists into balls and tried to breathe steadily.

'Don't do that. I don't want you to do that, Lorenzo. The time for that has long gone.' Her voice had sunk to a breathless whisper.

'Don't lie. You're enjoying this.' He raised her jumper and exposed her breast, covering the taut nipple with his mouth. She shuddered. She thought dazedly, We're enemies, but nothing was responding to reason.

She pressed his head against her and arched back as his mouth suckling against her breast sent volts of electricity through her body, through every nerve-ending.

'Tell me,' he murmured hoarsely, 'tell me about him. I need to know. Jeremy is dead and the past can no longer haunt you.'

'There's nothing to tell.' She pulled herself away, mortified at what had just happened as reality reasserted itself, and he drew back with a gesture of angry rejection.

'Damn you, Isobel,' he bit out, and she sprang off him, taking two steps backwards on shaky legs.

'You don't care about me, Lorenzo. What makes you think that I would ever confide in you? What makes you think that I would ever tell you about the past four years?' She laughed bitterly, hating him for arousing her and hating herself for her treacherous body.

'Oh, keep your bloody little secrets!' he said harshly, standing up, and she took a couple more steps backwards. He looked as though he was about to say more, his eyes like flint, his powerful body tensed with self-imposed control. But whatever more he had to say she didn't find out, because they both heard Mrs Chandler approaching and, in an automatic reaction, they both turned away from each other.

Isobel dragged a smile on to her face just as her mother walked through the door, but she still made sure that she didn't look at Lorenzo.

She was so overcome that she felt sick. Sick and giddy. As if she were suffering from some dreadful tropical disease that had infiltrated her whole system and left her incapable of coherent thought or action.

Wine had nothing to do with what had just taken place. It was as if a dam had burst and yearnings which she had spent years denying had surfaced, filling her and taking her over.

'All ready.' Her mother looked bright and alive. She took Lorenzo's arm, pressing him to tell her more about America, more about what he had been doing there. Isobel glanced at him from under her lashes and wondered whether his body was still throbbing the way that hers was, or whether his passion had died the minute she had pushed him away, the minute reality had shown him the face of the woman he now hated.

He said he wanted her and he did, but his hatred was more powerful than his desire. By marrying her he would satisfy both.

No one would think now, though, that he had anything on his mind other than an evening ahead of pleasant company and invigorating conversation.

The man, she thought, was an actor of the first order. He had always, even as a teenager, had the ability to conceal deep feeling, and that ability had obviously been honed to perfection over the years.

Isobel trailed behind them, feeling like a sulky schoolgirl at an adult gathering.

Her mother had laid the kitchen table, apologising in case Lorenzo thought it too informal, knowing that he would laugh warmly and make the right noises of appreciation. He did, and he really seemed to mean it.

Mrs Chandler had brought out a bottle of wine from the wine cellar and she handed it to Lorenzo, who opened it quickly and efficiently.

'Isobel hardly drinks at all, do you, darling? Tonight is the first time that I've seen her have more than one forced, polite glass of wine,' her mother said conversationally as he poured them each a glass, and Lorenzo raised his eyes in a question.

Immediately, and for no reason whatsoever, she felt on the defensive.

'I prefer not to,' she admitted carefully, sitting down and indulging in another sulky schoolgirl mannerism of toying with the cutlery. This was not like her at all. She had become cool, contained, virtually unflappable over the years. Where, she wondered, was all that now?

Lorenzo was looking at her; she could feel his eyes boring into her head, waiting for an elaboration on that statement. She had never been a heavy drinker when she knew him, but on the other hand she had not been averse to a glass of wine. In fact, she could think of countless times when they had cracked open a bottle and lain back, talking about nothing and everything, and she was quite certain that he remembered those occasions as well. He seemed to remember everything else.

'Jeremy——' her mother began, and Isobel cut in sharply.

'Mother!' He already knew, of course, that her marriage had not been a roaring success, but for some reason she was loath to confirm the depth of its failure. She didn't think that she could stand his pity as well as his contempt.

'He was fond of the odd glass now and then...?' Lorenzo pressed as he helped himself to a generous serving of chicken.

'More than the odd glass,' Mrs Chandler reflected, glancing quickly at her daughter.

'The vegetables,' Isobel stated in an over-loud voice, 'are home-grown.' There was no way that she wanted her mother to launch into the subject of Jeremy and his drinking. She knew that both her parents had been appalled and worried at his habit, which had steadily worsened over the years. At first they had made attempts to discuss it with both of them, then with her, since Jeremy became tight-lipped and defensive the minute it was mentioned as a problem, but she had laughingly joked the matter away, and after a while they had fallen silent on the subject. But she would have to have been blind not to notice their anxious glances at one another whenever she and Jeremy were around. They had found his behaviour distasteful, as she had. They had found *him* distasteful, but were too polite ever to mention it. But it had been there in their eyes, in glances caught when they thought that their daughter's attention was elsewhere.

No doubt her mother now thought that Lorenzo, as an old friend, was entitled to confidences on the subject, but Isobel was not about to fall into any such way of thinking.

'Mum,' she continued firmly, 'still maintains the vegetable plot at the back of the garden.' She concentrated heavily on the chicken on her plate. 'We have all kinds of herbs, green beans, potatoes. In summer the strawberries are marvellous.'

'In fact——' her mother was looking at Lorenzo and her face was sheepish but wistful '—and, darling, don't take this the wrong way, but just between the three of

us, David and I had always hoped——' she paused and
Isobel stared at her, horrified at some unformulated suspicion of what was to come '—had always thought that
you two…that you two would perhaps…who knows…?
Silly of us, wasn't it?' She smiled and so did Lorenzo,
a smile of triumph meant for Isobel's eyes only.

The smile of the victor.

CHAPTER SIX

THE subject was dropped as gracefully as it had arisen, but throughout the light-hearted chat about gardens Isobel could feel her head swimming with the desperate implications of her mother's remarks.

She had never, not once, mentioned any such thoughts to *her*. What on earth had possessed her to mention them now? In front of Lorenzo?

She looked at him, a sideways look, and wondered whether it was her imagination, or was a smile of satisfaction hovering on his lips?

She poured herself another glass of wine, throwing him a defiant look which met with an amused curve of his mouth, and only considered it safe to resurface back into the conversation when, inevitably, they began discussing old friends.

'Isobel tells me that Richard Adams is doing rather well,' Lorenzo murmured casually.

Probing, Isobel thought sourly. Did he want to find out from another source whether there was anything more to their relationship than she had told him? Did he think that they had carried on a torrid, clandestine affair behind Jeremy's back? She wouldn't have put it past him. In fact, there wasn't much she wouldn't put past him.

'What a nice young man,' Mrs Chandler said warmly. She looked at her daughter. 'You rather enjoy working with him, don't you, Isobel?'

'Immensely.' She noticed the slight frown on Lorenzo's face and smiled. 'He's bright, he's sympathetic, he's thoughtful.'

'A paragon, in other words,' Lorenzo said with an edge of coolness in his voice. 'How odd that he never married.'

'Waiting for the right woman,' Mrs Chandler said.

'How odd that *you* never married, Lorenzo,' Isobel said brightly. She sipped her wine and looked at him over the rim of her glass.

'Why?'

'Because you're free, single and, I suppose, quite eligible.'

'You think so?' he asked in that lazy, charming voice of his. He sat back and gave her the full brunt of his attention.

'I'm sure there are some women who would find you appealing,' Isobel replied, lowering her eyes. 'Especially in America. Don't women outnumber men over there?'

'Do they? I wasn't aware of that statistic.' He threw Mrs Chandler a semi-offended smile and said, reverting his attention back to Isobel, 'I'm not sure I like your back-handed compliment, that I'm only eligible because there's a surplus of women waiting to trap an unsuspecting man.'

Mrs Chandler laughed, which she was meant to, but there was a certain gentle calculation in her eyes that Isobel didn't care for.

'Anyway, I won't pry into your personal life, Lorenzo,' Isobel said briskly.

'Feel free. What would you like to know?'

'Nothing.'

'I find that difficult to believe. Surely you must be curious about me after four years.'

Mrs Chandler was watching them closely, with the amused half-smile of an adult watching the antics of two children, but that didn't fool Isobel. She knew her mother too well to be taken in by that bland, pleasant expression.

'No,' she said, hastily retreating from the conversation, and he shrugged, willing to let it go for the moment.

They had managed to proceed through the main course, and her mother now brought dessert to the table. An apple pie which, she felt compelled to admit, was left over from the day before.

They began chatting about Abigail—lustrous Abigail and her soaring career—and Isobel gradually relaxed. She was tremendously proud of her friend. She had done some plays on Broadway and Isobel grew voluble on the subject, comparing notes with Lorenzo, who had seen them both, laughing as the wine resumed its effect and they went over old times.

Talking over old times was safe, just so long as those old times didn't involve memories of Lorenzo, and they didn't.

He could be disarmingly witty and, by the time the apple pie had been consumed, any electricity in the atmosphere had evaporated.

Her mother began clearing away the dishes, and Lorenzo insisted that she relax in the sitting-room while he and Isobel tidied up the kitchen.

'The chef never washes,' he informed her, and she bustled away obligingly, leaving them alone in the kitchen.

'I feel as though I've drunk a case of wine,' Isobel said as she began washing. It felt good being here with him, in the warm, mellow kitchen with the blinds down and the chill autumn air blowing outside. Her caution seemed to have vanished.

'It agrees with you,' he said smoothly. 'You don't look as though you're permanently sharpening your weapons for a fight.'

'I'm not too sure I like that picture of myself,' she answered, laughing. 'You make me sound like a battle-axe.'

'Do I?' he asked softly from next to her. 'You're too damned beautiful ever to be described as a battle-axe. Battle-axes have iron-grey hair pinned into buns and enough wrinkles to tell the world just how dissatisfied they are with life.'

'Really?' She grinned to herself, and thought in a muddled way that she shouldn't be feeling happy, not here, not with him. 'I can't think that you've had much to do with grey-haired, wrinkled women who are dissatisfied with life.'

'What sort of women do you think I've had to do with?'

She plunged her hands into the soapy water and thought, at the back of her mind, that there was something dangerously exciting about this conversation.

'I have no idea.'

'Oh yes, you have,' he whispered huskily.

'Good-looking women, I suppose. Women who look stunning when they're draped on your arm.'

'I'm not interested in women as ornaments. I never have been. You of all people should know that.'

'Should I? Why?' She was so aware of him that she didn't dare lift her eyes to his.

'Do you consider yourself ornamental?'

She laughed nervously.

'This is not a conversation to have when I'm feeling light-headed,' she said, turning around with her back to

the kitchen sink, and he dropped the tea-cloth and faced
her, leaning to rest his hands on either side of her.

'What kind of conversation would you like?' he asked.
'Shall we talk about horticulture? Politics? The mating
habits of the beaver?'

She stared down at his hands and was aware that quite
a bit of her light-headedness was not due to the wine.
Her heart was beating fast, so fast that she felt as though
she were suffocating.

She looked at his strong hands, at the fine dark hair
curling over the watch-strap. She followed them up, her
eyes dwelling on the curve of his neck, the breadth of
his shoulders, and by the time they reached his face she
found that she was breathing quickly, gasping for air.

'Or shall we talk about something else, Isobel? Shall
we talk about Jeremy?'

'No. There's nothing to talk about. My life,' she added
in a whisper, 'has been nothing to talk about.'

Lorenzo didn't answer. He folded his arms around her
and drew her to him. She could hear the steady beat of
his heart as she rested her head against his chest and bit
back the sudden urge to cry.

'Oh, Isobel,' he murmured, stroking her hair. 'Was it
dreadful?'

She liked him stroking her hair like that. She so badly
wanted to be comforted.

'I miss my father dreadfully,' she whispered, incon-
sequentially, and he didn't say anything. He didn't have
to. He understood. She knew he did.

'Why won't you talk to me about it?' he asked roughly,
and she squeezed her eyes tightly shut. She heard him
sigh under his breath, but there wasn't the usual reaction
of fury. He just continued stroking her hair. Friends,
she thought, for the moment.

Except... She felt a quiver of real alarm. Except she didn't want his friendship, did she? It would be an impossible friendship anyway, because two people could never really reach each other when underneath there was an undercurrent of contempt and mistrust. Right now her defences had been lowered, she recognised that, and so, quite possibly, had his. He had, after all, had a few glasses of wine himself.

She drew back and looked straight into his face, and the realisation that she was looking at a man whom she still loved, whom she had never stopped loving, rocked her to her foundations.

She made a weak attempt to herself to rationalise that this stupid reaction was simply something born from unusual circumstances. Jeremy was no longer around, her father was no longer around—her dear father whom she had loved so much—but suddenly Lorenzo was, and nostalgia was playing its part in dictating emotions which, when she sat down and thought about them, didn't really exist.

But it was only a weak argument. She closed her eyes and knew that her heart had only ever belonged to one man. She had thrown away her chances with him because of necessity, and now there were no chances left because, at the end of the day, he hated her.

She took a deep, steadying breath and pushed past him.

She would have to be doubly careful now, she thought. If Lorenzo wanted to hurt her then he really wouldn't have to try very hard if he knew how she still felt about him.

Wouldn't that be the sweetest of poetic justice? she thought bitterly.

She fetched three cups from the cupboard, knowing that he was watching her.

'I take it that means that you don't want to talk to me about your marriage?'

'I told you,' Isobel mumbled, with her back to him, 'there's nothing to talk about.'

'In that case, why the secrecy?'

'Why can't you forget about what happened?' she asked. She heard the give-away desperation in her voice and covered it up by making a great fuss with the coffee-machine.

'He had something over you, didn't he?'

'What makes you say that?'

'You never loved him. No one who knew you seriously expected you to marry him. Abigail thought that for some reason you married him because you had to, you were compelled to——'

'Abigail?' She faced him swiftly. 'When were you talking to Abigail about me?'

'I went out to dinner with her after one of her plays.'

'She never told me. Why were you discussing me behind my back?'

'We weren't discussing you,' he answered tightly. 'There's no need to feel paranoid. We were talking about the past and you cropped up in the general conversation.'

'Oh, really?' Her voice was laden with scepticism. What had he been doing with Abigail? She felt a twinge of jealousy at the thought of the two of them, sitting in some cosy restaurant, smiling and exchanging confidences.

Abigail had never mentioned having seen him. Why? Had she had a fling with him and decided that discretion was the better part of valour?

'Oh, for God's sake,' he said roughly, 'I can see what's going through that head of yours, Isobel, and you're way off target.'

'Stop pretending that you know me!' she said, her voice high and sharp. 'Stop acting as though you can read my mind!'

'I've just told you that I had dinner with Abigail, a fact which she omitted to mention to you, and you're putting two and two together and coming up with six.'

'You can have dinner with whomever you choose,' Isobel informed him. 'Of course I'm surprised that she never mentioned it to me, but then she probably assumed, quite rightly, that I wouldn't be particularly interested.'

'No? Because your life here was too full?'

'This is stupid.' She turned away to find that her hands were trembling and her mind was filled with unpleasant, sour images of her best friend in bed with Lorenzo Cicolla.

'Has it occurred to you that she didn't mention anything because I happened to be with a woman when I met her for dinner?'

'I see.'

'Maybe she felt a little awkward talking about me in connection with a woman. Maybe she felt that, as my ex-lover, you might be a little taken aback.'

Isobel laughed shortly. 'Why? Why would she feel that? I had my own life here.'

'If you call marriage to Jeremy a life.'

'You have no idea what sort of life we had together!'

'I can guess.'

'And of course you'd be right, wouldn't you?' she said acidly. 'After four years of absence you swan back here, make your deductions, and of course the infallible Lorenzo Cicolla would be absolutely spot-on!'

'You didn't love him. It was obvious on the day you married him. Why would that change?'

There was a tautness about his mouth when he said that.

'Answer me!' he muttered, taking a step towards her. 'You never cared for him, did you? And neither did your parents. He was a bully as a boy and the trait never deserted him. He drank, and God only knows what else he did. Run around with other women?'

'Stop it, Lorenzo!'

'Why? Why should I stop it? I want you to tell me why you married him.'

His eyes flared dangerously and she wondered, in dry-mouthed panic, how passion could turn to hatred like this.

'It's in the past,' she muttered. 'Forget it.'

'There's no getting through to you, is there, Isobel?' he asked, putting his hands on her shoulders, and she felt his fingers bite into her skin. 'You make noises about forgetting the past but, tell me, would you? If I had walked out on you then, when we were lovers, would you be prepared to smile forgivingly through it?'

'I suppose not,' Isobel said, looking down miserably.

'Then why,' he asked in a cold, brutal voice, 'do you imagine for a moment that I should?'

'Because there's no point dwelling on it, is there?'

His mouth twisted. 'And would you be mouthing all this now if I had returned empty-handed? No money in the coffers?'

'Of course.'

'Oh, I'm sure,' he sneered, and she flinched away from the look in his eyes. 'After four years I've become eligible, haven't I, Isobel? Why don't you admit it? Maybe Abigail was wrong, maybe you'd *like* me to believe that there was some dark, ulterior motive for marrying him because the truth is just too sordid. Is that it? The truth being that you married him because you wanted to make a match with someone you considered to be of the same social standing as yourself. The fact that we had been lovers was nothing more than an inconvenience.'

'Believe what you want,' she answered stubbornly.

It was like waving a red rag at a bull. His eyes glittered with savage fury and he shook her, really shook her, like a rag doll.

'You used me, Isobel,' he said through gritted teeth. 'What were you thinking when you touched me? What did you feel when we made love? That this was all something casual, a bit of a laugh? That I just wasn't rich enough for you? No more than a poor Italian boy with his poor Italian parents?'

'No!'

'Small towns breed insularity,' he muttered, ignoring her protest, his eyes burning into hers. His fingers were still biting into her flesh. In the morning there would be bruises, she thought. 'Small towns with small minds.'

'That being the case, why are you here?'

He looked at her and she felt unsteadied by his light, mesmeric eyes. 'You made a big mistake thinking that you could play with me, Isobel. No one plays with me. Do you understand? I went to America and I made my fortune, and now I have returned and here I shall stay. I will have your father's company and I will have you.'

'I won't marry you!'

He laughed coldly and his hand moved to caress the nape of her neck, his fingers soft although there was no gentleness in the gesture.

'How can you take pleasure in this?' she asked, but he didn't need to provide an answer to that one. 'You're crazy,' she muttered, wishing that he would remove himself to another part of the kitchen so that she could, at least breathe properly. The feel of his fingers on her neck was making her hair stand on end.

'Surely you have to admit that marriage would have its compensations, Isobel?' he said in a husky voice. 'You want me to make love to you as much as I want to.' He ran his fingers along her spine and her body froze as his hand found her breast. 'You see,' he whispered, rubbing her nipple with his thumb, feeling it swell to his touch, 'you can't fight me. I mean to have my way.'

'You would marry me simply for revenge? I'm not a possession, Lorenzo.' His finger continued to rub the throbbing bud of her breast and she could feel her face burning. He bent to kiss her neck, pulling her head back with his free hand.

They were both breathing heavily and when he pulled her against him, his hands moving to encircle her waist, she felt the hardness of his arousal with a shiver of longing.

'Shame,' he said coolly, smiling down at her, 'the place isn't quite right for making love, is it?'

Isobel pulled away from him and fled to the corner of the kitchen, grabbing up a tray and sticking it in front of her like a shield.

'Why don't you go into the sitting-room?' she asked on a high note.

'And let you get yourself in order?' He was still smiling. 'You do look a little ruffled.'

'I'm so glad you're enjoying yourself,' she said tightly. 'And what,' she added, on the spur of the moment, 'would your woman friend think if she could see you now? Or was the woman Abigail failed to mention no more than a passing fancy?'

He laughed. 'I thought you weren't curious about me?'

'I've always been curious about a man who is willing to sleep with two women at the same time,' she said, thinking on her feet.

The tray was beginning to feel heavy, but suddenly it didn't matter. She wanted desperately to hear about this woman. Jealousy clawed through her with sickening speed and she hated herself for it. Four years of bitter experience had not made her older and wiser, she thought, it had made her more stupid.

'Jessica,' he said, moving to relieve her of the tray, and talking in a normal voice as though, Isobel thought, discussing his damned sex-life was on a par with discussing the weather. 'She's blonde, beautiful, and she's my accountant. Satisfied?'

He walked towards the door with Isobel trailing behind him, her arms folded across her chest.

Beautiful and brainy. He had told her that he was not attracted to ornaments. Her imagination threw up at her images of a tall, leggy model who could converse about high finance with ease, and she felt slightly ill. And not in the least satisfied.

'And is she pining for you back in America?' she asked sweetly, addressing his back.

He stopped abruptly and she nearly careered into him. He was smiling with satisfied amusement.

'I knew you wouldn't let go of that topic so quickly.'

'Oh, you knew, did you?' She blushed and met his eyes with what she hoped was a steady stare.

'Of course I did. You forget——' he leaned slightly towards her, still smiling '—I know you well. You always were one to hammer away at something until you were completely satisfied. I remember a certain occasion when I arrived late to see you one evening and, despite the fact that you professed no interest whatsoever in my reasons, you gnawed away until I'd explained it all to you, right down to which side of the car the flat tyre had been on.'

That made her redden even more. It also rendered her temporarily speechless.

In one casual sentence he had sent her whirling back through time, to when life was full of heady optimism. It hurt all the more when she forced herself back to the present and back to the realisation that heady optimism was a lifetime away.

'To answer your question,' he continued in a casual voice, 'I have no idea whether Jessica is pining my absence. She has an extremely full life, an extremely demanding job and she's probably too exhausted in the evening to spend much time doing anything, including pining.'

'I'm staggered that you could tear yourself away from such an invigorating woman,' Isobel replied on a sour note. Her imagination had now elevated this other woman from merely being bright to being a positive genius, the sort who filled what little spare time she possessed pursuing some highly intellectual interest—like brain surgery.

'So am I,' he mused.

'Then why do you?' she snapped. 'Heathrow is well-stocked with planes going to America.'

'I told you,' Lorenzo said coldly, 'you won't be getting rid of me. I have business here, and I shall stay here until it is completed.'

Their eyes met in hostile understanding.

'You would give up a woman you love simply to satisfy some warped desire for revenge?' she asked on an indrawn breath.

Lorenzo didn't say anything for a while. When he finally spoke, his voice was a lazy drawl.

'Whoever mentioned giving up anyone? You'll meet Jessica yourself in due course. She's going to be coming out here to work for me.'

'You're going to bring . . . You intend to . . .'

'Stuck for words, Isobel?'

'You disgust me.' She half turned and he said viciously, under his breath,

'I didn't notice such scruples when you walked out on me to marry Jeremy Baker. Or don't the rules of the game apply to yourself?'

'I had my reasons,' she muttered.

'What? What were they?' There was a savage urgency in his voice, and in the hard contours of his face.

'The coffee's getting cold,' she mumbled, looking away, and he turned on his heel, his mouth drawn into a tight line of anger.

Her skin felt as though it were on fire. She could see now what game he intended to play. The pieces of the jigsaw were falling into place.

He wanted her to marry him, to have her tied to his side, the possession that was once denied him; but on the sidelines he would have his mistress, this other woman.

He didn't know that she still loved him. If he knew that, then where would she be? She wouldn't let herself be hurt again. Hadn't she suffered enough? she thought with anguish. She would never marry him. Sooner or later, he would have to give up.

She followed him into the lounge where her mother, thank goodness, had not dropped off to sleep or anything inconvenient like that. She had refused to have sleeping tablets when her husband had died, was still sleeping badly most nights, and consequently had developed a habit of nodding off in the armchair in the sitting-room.

'My, you two took a long time in the kitchen,' she said mildly when they entered, and Isobel gave her a warning look which was blithely ignored.

'Did we?' Lorenzo deposited the tray on the coffee-table and shot Isobel a sideways look from under his lashes as Mrs Chandler leaned forward to pour the coffee.

'Mmm.' She handed Lorenzo his cup. 'Not that I mind.' She handed Isobel her cup. 'I'm sure it does Isobel the world of good having an old friend to talk to.'

Isobel stifled a laugh at that one and sipped her coffee.

'Abigail,' Mrs Chandler sighed, 'is always on the road.'

'An itinerant life,' Lorenzo murmured obligingly, settling back into the chair as though in no hurry to see the front door.

'So it's refreshing for her to have you around, Lorenzo, I'm sure.' She looked at her daughter. 'Isn't it, darling?'

'Oh, extremely,' Isobel muttered. About as refreshing as bathing in a sheep-dip.

'That's nice to hear, Isobel,' Lorenzo said with a wicked grin.

'I do hope,' Mrs Chandler continued in the same pensive voice, 'that working together to sort out David's company will be possible.'

'So do I,' Lorenzo said, with rather more significance in his voice, which Isobel had no difficulty in picking up but which her mother happily missed.

'It will be so very nice to have you around, Lorenzo.' She paused and appeared to search around for the right words. 'Especially since I've decided to visit an old relative in Cornwall for a few weeks.'

'Old relative?' Isobel nearly gagged on a mouthful of coffee. 'Cornwall? What on earth are you talking about, Mother?'

'Haven't I mentioned it to you?'

'You know you haven't.'

'Oh dear, I meant to, but things have been so hectic here, what with all this business over the company.'

'What relative, Mother?' Isobel persisted. 'You can't possibly mean Aunt Dora?'

'I haven't seen her in absolutely ages, and she's always been so terribly keen to have us down.'

'She drives you crazy. She fusses.'

'She's just recovering from an operation, you know,' she said confidentially to Lorenzo. 'Her hip. Poor old thing.'

'She has a home help,' Isobel pointed out.

'But a relative would be so much nicer for her, don't you think, darling?' Mrs Chandler smiled. 'I may not be the most speedy thing in the world with my illness, but I can make a passable cup of tea and we're both so interested in the same things. Gardening, books.' She sighed. 'It will do me good, Isobel. I need to get away from here, to have a break from this house, with its memories.'

Isobel looked at her mother helplessly.

'But now?' she asked. 'Why now?'

'Why not?'

'I think it's a splendid idea,' Lorenzo said, and Isobel glowered at him.

How dared he contribute to a conversation which had nothing to do with him?

She looked at her mother, serenely sipping from her cup of coffee.

This *didn't* have anything to do with him, did it? Her mother couldn't possibly be indulging in a spot of matchmaking, could she?

She subsided into frowning, thoughtful silence, and only heard her mother's question as a vague murmur to Lorenzo in the background.

'Where are you staying?'

'In a hotel,' Lorenzo said, surprised by the question. 'The Edwardian on the outskirts of the town. Time cer-

tainly hasn't smiled kindly there.' He contemplated Mrs
Chandler over the rim of the cup while Isobel only absentmindedly tuned in to what they were saying.

She was managing quite nicely to persuade herself that
there was nothing ulterior in her mother's sudden decision to go and visit Dora Gately, who was a sweet old
biddy and was, in truth, recuperating from an operation
on her hip. They had not seen each other for quite some
time and Cornwall would be relaxing for her mother.

'Those poor people,' Mrs Chandler was saying. 'He
drinks, you know, old Albert Towser. It's no great secret
but he drank away a lot of the profit the place made in
the boom years, and now, when belts need to be
tightened, they're finding themselves terribly stretched.
They're thinking of selling. The business is simply no
longer there. Two factories have shut down since you
were here, and there is just no call for a hotel of that
size. In addition to which, the place is in a terrible state
from all accounts. And, of course, no money at all to
do the necessary repair work.'

Isobel had moved on from the knotty problem of
wondering what her mother's motives were and was now
debating whether she couldn't migrate to some other part
of the world, if Lorenzo Cicolla proved to be as disas-
trously persistent as he intended to be. They said that
the sun always shone in Australia. Wishful thinking, of
course, since she would never dream of leaving her
mother.

'The food's gone downhill as well,' Mrs Chandler was
continuing to muse. 'Alice used to do quite a bit of the
cooking, and she *always* supervised the kitchens, but
she's had her hands full with Albert these past few years
and she's no longer a young woman herself.'

France, Isobel thought, was closer to England, but far
from Yorkshire. Maybe her mother would consider the

South of France. It was sunny there as well. No, perhaps not. What would happen to the physiotherapy course she wanted to start on later in the year? Her French left a lot to be desired.

'The food *is* pretty poor,' Lorenzo was agreeing conversationally. 'Not,' he added loyally, 'like this little establishment here—even if the apple pie's a day old.' He grinned teasingly.

Dorset. The weather would be rubbish, Isobel reflected, but there would be no Lorenzo Cicolla making her life hell and, far away from him, she could cure herself of her foolish love.

One thing was certain, she couldn't stay here and she couldn't bank on his leaving simply because she refused to marry him. He might decide to buy her father's firm, without her consent to marry him, and then while away his time dogging her every move while his leggy, blonde mistress warmed his bed on the sidelines.

'Which is why,' she heard her mother say firmly, 'and especially now that I have decided to spend some time with Dora, I think you ought to come here to stay. At least until you've found yourself a place of your own.'

At which point Isobel tuned in with horror to the gist of a conversation which had been wafting over her for the past fifteen minutes.

'You can be company,' Mrs Chandler said with a comfortable smile on her lovely face, 'for Isobel.'

CHAPTER SEVEN

ISOBEL lay on the bed and stared upwards at the ceiling. The light was switched off, so she couldn't see anything in the dark, but there was no way that she could close her eyes. She would never get to sleep anyway.

'How,' she had asked her mother an hour previously, after she had sat through arrangements between Lorenzo and her mother in a stunned silence, 'could you have invited him to stay *here*?' Lorenzo had already left, to return the following afternoon.

'It seemed logical,' Mrs Chandler had answered, standing up and heading towards her bedroom. Isobel had followed in her wake, trying to be calm. 'After all, the house is huge—much too big for just the two of us. And with me gone to stay with your aunt, you would just rattle around here. It would worry me.'

'Why? I'm fine with my own company. I don't need...'

'I would feel happier knowing that Lorenzo was here.' She had paused outside her bedroom door, and Isobel had pointedly ignored the implication that the discussion was finished, at least until the following morning.

'But this is *our* house, and Lorenzo Cicolla is——' she was close to spluttering '—a *stranger*! And to cap it all, you're going to go away and leave me...us...here!' She was spluttering and beginning to sound like a plaintive child and her mother smiled indulgently.

'He's hardly a stranger, darling. Anyone would think that you'd never laid eyes on him before,' her mother had reproved, pulling back the bedspread and then sitting down at the dressing-table to remove her make-up. 'I

117

don't know what's come over you all of a sudden, Isobel. I know you're still fraught after Jeremy's death, and your dad's. We both are. But you were very rude this evening.'

'I wasn't rude,' Isobel had said stubbornly. 'I just don't think it's a good idea to throw open the doors to any and everyone who happens to be passing by.'

'Lorenzo is an old friend!' She had faced her daughter. 'I thought it might have helped you. I thought, darling, that the company would be good for you. You're far too inclined to retreat into yourself. Besides, if you two are thrown together it might knock some sense into both of you, get you working together so that Lorenzo can go ahead and settle the deal on your father's firm. You used to be such close friends—more than that. I simply don't know what's going on here.'

And that, Isobel now thought, had been the end of that.

Lorenzo was going to be moving in. Of course she could have moved out herself, but then that would have seemed like running away, and besides, the thought of moving back into her own house, *Jeremy*'s house, as she had always considered it, wasn't appealing. She didn't know if she could face being surrounded by memories of the unhappiness that had been forced upon her, memories of the silence, the despair born out of secrets which should have remained buried in the past.

She lay in bed, seething, and when she awoke the following morning, she was heavy-eyed and bad-tempered.

It didn't help that her mother seemed thrilled at the prospect of Lorenzo coming to stay. With what seemed to Isobel indecent haste, she had packed her bags and consulted train timetables. She would leave that evening and Aunt Dora was going to have some late tea laid on, and wasn't that wonderful, my sweet, oh, it *will* be restful.

Isobel departed for the surgery on her bicycle with dark thoughts. If she happened to bump into Lorenzo Cicolla, then she would give him a piece of her mind, because she had been too taken aback the evening before to do much more than stare at them both in open-mouthed horror.

She didn't, though. She spent a tiring day at the surgery and emerged at five o'clock into a depressingly cold drizzle of rain.

Lorenzo was outside. He seemed, she thought antagonistically, to make a habit of accosting her outside her work.

She debated whether to pretend that she hadn't seen his car parked across the road, and while she was busy debating he stepped out and sprinted across the road towards her.

It was cold, and he was wearing a long black coat over his suit, which seemed to emphasise his height and muscularity.

'I hoped I might catch you before you left,' he said, not giving her time to say anything. 'I want to have a few words with you.'

'It's raining.'

'So I've noticed. Come on.'

This time she didn't try to protest. What would have been the point? He would have steamrollered her along with him like the last time anyway.

She wheeled her bicycle along the pavement, putting it between the two of them, hurrying to keep up with him.

She was soaked by the time they made it to the pub.

'You're wet,' Tom said, as if pointing out something that might have escaped them.

'Very perceptive, Tom,' Isobel muttered. 'Coffee would be nice.'

He went off to get their order and returned, saying with his usual forthrightness, 'Seems to be getting a habit, this, doesn't it? You two having a drink together.'

It was impossible to get annoyed with Tom. His bluntness was too disarming.

'We keep running into one another,' Lorenzo said, not looking at her. 'Hazards of small-town living, I guess.'

Tom nodded. 'If you could call it a hazard,' he replied, with a great deal of philosophical insight for him. 'I like it myself.' He pointed towards the table where they had last sat. 'Your table's empty. Nice and cosy too, in front of the fire. I'll bring coffee along when it's ready.'

'*Our* table?' Isobel hissed to Lorenzo once they were out of earshot. 'We've only been here twice, for heaven's sake!'

Lorenzo lowered his body into the chair and looked at her through his lashes. 'In a place this size, twice constitutes a habit.'

Tom approached them with the coffee, and they made polite noises about the weather. He himself lived above the pub with his wife and children, but his brother had a modest farm on the outskirts of the village, and consequently Tom was something of a self-proclaimed expert on the weather and its effects on various types of vegetables and livestock.

Isobel listened while he and Lorenzo conversed and, as soon as he was gone, she turned to Lorenzo and said furiously, not bothering to hide behind politeness, 'How could you?'

'How could I what?'

'You know what! How could you accept my mother's invitation to stay at the house? Especially knowing that she wasn't going to be around!'

'Nothing like coming to the point, is there?' He sipped from his glass, then carefully put it down on the table. 'But I'm glad you brought the subject up because that's precisely what I wanted to talk to you about.'

'Snap!' Isobel looked at his unsmiling face mutinously. She had had a good few hours to consider the situation, and her thoughts on the matter hadn't become any more accepting.

How was she ever going to stand having him around her, under the same roof? Without even the comforting third presence of her mother?

'You're acting like a child,' Lorenzo said coolly, and she could have hit him.

'Me? A child?' She swallowed a mouthful of coffee and then cradled the cup in her hands. 'You really want to make life as difficult as possible for me, don't you?' she asked bitterly.

'Your mother would have been hurt if I had rejected her offer. She wants this deal with your father's company to go through, which is one reason why she's throwing us together. And anyway, as far as she is concerned, why should I stay in a draughty, uncomfortable hotel room when her own house is so vast?'

It made sense, of course, but that only made Isobel angrier.

'Because you're out of my hair when you're in a draughty, uncomfortable hotel room.'

'Don't be so damned self-centred.'

'You can stay in *my* house,' she offered, clutching a sudden safety belt, and his brows met in a black frown.

'Are you quite mad?' he asked smoothly.

'It's empty!'

'Not for me, it isn't.' He swallowed a long mouthful of his drink and looked at her savagely. 'And the reason I wanted to see you before I moved in was to warn you to stop acting as though you want to kill me in front of your mother. She's going away to relax, and why don't you just allow her that sensible piece of freedom without having to worry that she'll return to find a corpse on her hands? That will achieve nothing more than unnecessarily upsetting her.'

'Don't tell me what's going to upset my mother!'

'I damn well will, because right now you're not seeing further than your own nose. I'm moving in and that's a fact, so you might as well grin and bear it.'

'I'd rather grin and bear a nuclear war,' she said through gritted teeth, and he laughed, relaxing back in the chair and giving her a long, appreciative look. Isobel reddened and said quickly, 'Why did you sell your mother's house if you had plans to return to England?'

Lorenzo looked at her thoughtfully. 'Because I had no idea when I would return, or, to be honest, where I would live.'

'Until events propelled you back to this little place.' The bitterness had crept back into her voice.

He shrugged. 'At any rate, it seemed foolish to continue maintaining an unoccupied house.'

'So I take it you're actively looking for somewhere to live?'

'Do I detect a note of optimism in your voice?' he asked lazily.

She didn't like it when he was like this, when the charm was lurking so close to the surface. He was untrustworthy, she had to remind herself, and he was hell-bent on hurting her. She glanced at him from under her lashes. Why hadn't the passing years turned him into an unappealing, overweight businessman? Maybe she wouldn't have found her senses doing somersaults if he wasn't so damned sexy.

'Curiosity,' she answered at last, and he raised his eyebrows.

'Well, to satisfy your curiosity, yes, I shall be looking for somewhere to live. Any suggestions?'

'That depends on the kind of house that you're looking for.'

'What would you recommend?'

'I don't know your tastes,' she replied succinctly.

'Don't you?'

She was beginning to feel breathless.

'I don't know what you can afford,' she said, avoiding the question and he laughed.

'I can afford anything.'

'Your best bet is to go along to John Evans on the High Street and find out what they've got.' She began making fiddly movements to indicate that she was ready to leave.

'Yes, you could do that, couldn't you?' he murmured softly, amused at her tight-lipped reaction to that.

'No.'

'Why not? You know my taste in houses, whether you want to admit it or not. Didn't we spend idle hours discussing where we'd live if we ever settled down together?'

Disastrous things were happening to her equilibrium. She didn't want to remember the past with him; she didn't want to confront the awful comparison between what they had then and what they had now.

'Right now,' he said smoothly, 'I haven't got time to visit properties.'

'Why not?'

'I have to establish a working base here so that I can communicate with my other companies, before I get down to your father's, that is.'

'Over my dead body.'

'Jessica will be bringing over paperwork, and I shall have to install a fax machine.'

'Surely the wondrous Jessica would be able to do all that and give you ample time to find your own house? From what you say, she could run a business single-handed in between raising ten children and knocking out gourmet meals in the length of time it would take most normal people to open a can of beans.'

'Jealous?'

'Hardly.'

'You could have done something with your life, Isobel. You were destined to.' He leaned forward urgently. 'Greatness was expected from you. How could you have been satisfied with anything less?'

'Not everyone lives up to their expectations.' Her words were practically inaudible. She didn't want to talk about this and her lowered eyes and set mouth said as much.

'And there ends the subject?'

'I haven't got time to house-hunt on your behalf,' she said, ending the subject.

'On *our* behalf,' he said with smiling, steely-eyed menace. 'And I rather think you have. After all, wouldn't you like me out of here so that you can come to terms, in privacy, with the inevitable?'

He looked at her and smiled, knowing that he had trapped her.

'I'll think about it,' Isobel mumbled, standing up. She couldn't quite explain it to herself, but she felt uneasy about becoming involved in something as personal as choosing a house for Lorenzo Cicolla. It felt as though she was beginning the process of giving in to his demands, but he was right: living under the same roof as him was going to drive her insane, and she easily had more time than he had to hunt around properties.

'You'd better come back with me,' Lorenzo said as they went outside to find that the drizzle was now bordering on a downpour. He took her bike and ran towards his car, with her following him.

They were both dripping once more by the time they were inside the car. He started the engine, turned on the windscreen wipers, and it was only when they had been driving for a while that she realised that they were not headed in the right direction for her mother's house.

Her body jerked up in panic and she said, in a rushed voice, 'Where are we going?'

'The Edwardian.'

'What for?'

He looked at her sideways. 'To collect my things. Clothes, papers, my computer terminal. Any objections?'

Isobel tried to look nonchalant in the dark, but she was nervous by the time they arrived at the hotel. When he had first arrived, she had assumed, blithely, that she could more or less avoid having any contact with him, but here she was now, about to face the prospect of sharing her mother's house with him, not to mention scouring estate agents on his behalf.

The Edwardian was a large hotel on the outskirts of the town, and it was obvious that it must have been quite something in its heyday. Unfortunately, as her mother had said, its heyday had long since vanished, and as they walked into the foyer she was all too aware of those little tell-tale signs of a place that has hit on hard times. The paint needed updating, the wallpaper needed updating—even the furniture dotted about here and there looked as though it had seen much better days.

Mrs Towser was standing behind the reception desk and she looked harassed.

'So sorry to hear about your father and your husband, dear,' she said to Isobel as Lorenzo settled his bill. She looked slyly across to him. 'Your house must seem very empty without your husband around.'

'I'm staying with my mother,' Isobel answered shortly. She didn't want to encourage an interrogation from Mrs Towser, so she looked vacantly around her.

'Yes, dear. A very good idea.' She ceased looking curious, and her expression of harassment reappeared. Isobel got the feeling that she was so wrapped up in her own worries that she had little time to concern herself with other people.

Lorenzo handed her the cheque, which she perfunctorily glanced at, and it was a relief to escape the atmosphere of doom which pervaded the area around the desk.

There was no lift. They walked along a network of corridors, through archways, up some stairs, and finally arrived at the room.

'I'll wait for you outside, shall I?' Isobel suggested as he pushed open the door, and Lorenzo said with his back to her,

'Don't be ridiculous. I don't know how long I shall be. There's no point standing out there in the freezing corridor.' So she reluctantly entered and resumed her inspection of the hotel décor while he threw his things into suitcases.

Her parents had used to come here, occasionally, for Sunday lunch when she was a child. It had always been something of a treat. It seemed sad to think that the place was now a shabby building with all glamour and elegance long stripped from it.

He had finished packing. He briefly glanced around to make sure that he was not forgetting anything, then moved to the door, where she had been standing in silence for the past fifteen minutes.

'There,' he said, leaning against the door and surveying her with a certain amount of cool amusement, 'all done, and you're unscathed by the experience.'

Isobel didn't answer. She rested her hand meaningfully on the door-knob and he covered it with his. Immediately her body froze.

'Why were you so reluctant to come here with me, Isobel?' he asked mockingly. 'Did you think that I might be overcome with lust if I found myself in a bedroom with you?'

'Perish the thought,' she said promptly.

'Of course, I'll admit that there was a time...' He coiled his fingers in her hair and she looked up at him with a small, inaudible gasp. The room seemed to be closing in and she found that she was perspiring slightly.

She had no idea how long they stayed like that, staring at each other. What was he thinking? His expression was shuttered but there was an unspoken feverish heat about him that radiated from his body.

Her eyes drifted down to his mouth, and his fingers tightened in her hair until he was hurting her.

What was needed now, she thought, was banality. She should say something, anything, to break the intense erotic atmosphere between them, but she couldn't get a word out.

She found herself straining towards him, wanting him with a depth of desire that knocked the breath out of her body.

She wanted his mouth to cover hers, she wanted his hands to explore her body, she wanted to feel the burning, sensual passion which she had known with him years before, in that age of innocence.

'Damn you, Isobel,' he said fiercely. His hand dropped and he pulled open the door.

He had wanted her, she thought numbly, following him out into the corridor. He had wanted her as badly just then as she had wanted him, but the past had come between them, that terrible secret which was like a chasm stretching into infinity.

They drove to her mother's house in a tense silence. Mrs Chandler was waiting for them. She had cooked, Isobel thought sourly, probably something special. The aroma wafted from the kitchen, and Lorenzo, she jealously noticed, switched automatically into charming mode, delighting her mother. Naturally.

'Such a wet night,' Mrs Chandler was saying. 'I thought a lovely hotpot. Though not for me. I have a taxi booked to take me to the station shortly.'

'I would have dropped you,' Lorenzo said quickly, frowning, and Mrs Chandler waved aside his protest. 'You shouldn't have gone to any trouble,' he murmured, smiling, and Isobel chipped in acidly,

'No. You shouldn't.'

Her mother pretended not to notice. She glanced down at Lorenzo's suitcases and began chatting to him about the lack of luggage.

'If you had been a woman,' she mused, walking into the hall, which was beautifully warm after the damp cold of the hotel room, 'you would have come with several trunks! Isn't that so, darling?' She looked at Isobel, who stretched her lips into a stony smile.

'I think I'll go and have a bath,' she said by way of response.

'Oh, yes. You're both rather like drowned rats!'

Isobel scowled and wished that her mother wouldn't address them both as though they were a couple of delightful children.

'Darling,' she turned to her daughter, 'do show Lorenzo up to his room. You know which one he's having.'

'Yes.' And if I forget, she told herself, I can always follow the scent of the freshly picked flowers.

She led the way, not looking back to see if he was following her, hoping that he would perhaps trip over one of his suitcases and find himself another landlady courtesy of the local hospital, but naturally he didn't. He was too strong and too graceful a mover for any such clumsy misadventure.

'Here you go.' She pushed open the bedroom door and turned to go, but his hand snapped out, curling around hers, and he said to her half-averted face,

'Watch it, Isobel. Think about your mother and not yourself.' He let her go and she fled to her own bedroom, which was just along the corridor.

Once inside the room, she leaned back against the closed door and made an effort to think calm, peaceful thoughts. If she was going to react like this, she would be a wreck inside a week. She would have to grin and bear his presence and do her damnedest to make sure that he didn't get an inkling as to what was going on inside her.

She had a quick bath, and emerged feeling not much more refreshed than before she went in.

She had wrapped her towel around her and she absent-mindedly began flicking through her wardrobe, her thoughts elsewhere.

She would have to find a house for him to live in as soon as possible. She was due some holiday and she would take it and spend the time narrowing down the possibilities. She wondered whether it could all be accomplished in the space of a day.

Nine a.m.: go to estate agents. Ten a.m.: start looking. Five p.m.: finish looking. Six p.m.: inform him that she had found something suitable. Goodbye.

She didn't hear the door being pushed open. She was too furiously concentrating on her plan of action, so when she looked into the mirror and saw his reflection staring back at her she almost hit the ceiling.

'What are you doing here?' she asked breathlessly, clutching the towel around her.

'No towel.'

'Airing cupboard.' Her feet were glued to the ground and a feeling of panic rose into her throat as he closed the door quietly behind him and took a few steps towards her.

'Out!'

He was standing right in front of her and she wished that she had had the forethought to put on her bathrobe instead of this ineffectual little towel which barely covered her body. But then she hadn't expected him to barge into her bedroom, had she?

'I don't want you here!' she said, looking up at him.

'Do you think I want to be here?' he grated.

Her mouth parted, and he lowered his head. She knew what his intentions were even before he kissed her, but she was still shocked when she felt his lips crush hers. His tongue invaded the inside of her mouth with hunger and a little groan escaped from her throat.

His hands moved to the small of her back, pressing her against him.

She could feel the urgency of his arousal, hard against her, and her limbs began to melt.

'No!' Her voice was muffled against his mouth.

'Yes! Damn you!' He pulled her head back and kissed her throat, then lifted her and carried her across to the bed.

There was nothing gentle about him. The lines of his face were hard, aggressive, but his eyes were on fire.

She was still clutching the towel, and he pulled her hands away, pinning them above her head.

'Lorenzo!' She said his name in a shaking, husky voice, with her eyes closed. It seemed like a million years ago that she had felt this wild, reckless passion soaring through her, and as the towel fell open she arched her body up, so that her breasts could receive the moist exploration of his mouth.

She wanted him so badly that she was aching all over, so badly that she couldn't think at all, never mind think straight.

His tongue flicked over one hardened nipple and she shuddered. He took her breasts in his hands and she pressed his dark head against her, watching him as he suckled her nipples.

When he shifted to trail his tongue along her stomach she moaned, and writhed against him.

This was what she had been so afraid of. This awful, compulsive reaction, this desperate needing that had never left her. All through her long marriage to Jeremy she had kept on wanting Lorenzo. It had been a steady beat drumming at the back of her mind.

His tongue found the moist centre between her legs, and as it darted into the sweet core of her being she had to stop herself from whimpering aloud.

'Make love to me, Lorenzo,' she groaned, and he raised his head to look at her. Their eyes tangled, and with a sharp movement he stood up. It was like being cocooned under a warm blanket, only to find it snatched away from you. Isobel sat up and looked at him with bewildered eyes.

Reality hadn't quite hit her as yet. Her body was still throbbing.

'Get up,' he said shortly, and that was when reality struck her in the face. She pulled the towel around her and struggled to her feet, because lying there on the bed made her feel intensely vulnerable.

'Lorenzo...!' she began, and his voice was like a whiplash.

'When I take you, Isobel—and I will—it will be in *our* house. You will be *mine*, not on temporary loan but with a ring on your finger. You made love with me once and then married another man. Damn you, Isobel Chandler, the next time I will have you, and there will be no running away!' There was angry intent on his face and she wished that the ground would open up and swallow her whole. She couldn't find a thing to say.

He spun around on his heel and she watched in silence as he left the bedroom, quietly shutting the door behind him. Then she collapsed on to the bed, shaking.

So this was how their story ended. Anger where love should have been. She began to cry, steadily and silently, until she felt too weary to shed any more tears. Then she washed her face and applied her make-up carefully. She didn't want her mother to see that she had been crying. She didn't want Lorenzo to see that she had been crying. She would let him believe that she was fine, hunky-dory, that she too could put the whole thing down to experience, a regrettable incident.

She felt wooden as she made her way downstairs, and it was with deep relief that she was granted a temporary reprieve from him. He was still upstairs. That gave her time to get herself together.

Her mother was in the kitchen. She had made some home-made bread to take with her. Did that seem a good idea? She had also bought some smoked salmon. She was sure that Aunt Dora would love that. Was that all right? She thought it nicer than flowers.

Isobel nodded and answered and wondered miserably where all those silver linings on those clouds had gone.

She didn't look around when Lorenzo walked in, although she felt a chill run down her spine. Her mother was glancing at her watch and chatting, but with one ear open for the sound of the doorbell.

Lorenzo regarded her expressionlessly, and she looked back at him in like manner. Two ships that had once crossed in the night, but were now on impossibly parallel paths.

'I thought that I might start looking at houses for you tomorrow,' she said politely. 'Lorenzo has asked me to help him house-hunt,' she explained, turning to her mother.

'I think that's an excellent idea,' Mrs Chandler said. 'What sort of place are you looking for?'

'Old,' Lorenzo said, turning away from Isobel. If body language said something, she thought, then it was speaking volumes right now, because the twist of his body was telling her as clearly as if he had written the message in neon lettering on the table that although he might want her, beyond that there was nothing but scathing dislike. 'I rather like Tudor-style houses, and my mother absolutely insists on a garden.'

Mrs Chandler nodded approvingly. 'I see her point. There's Bearwood Cottage up for sale. I know that through Emily. Mrs Jenkins is moving down to Surrey to live with one of her daughters.'

Mrs Chandler carried on talking, discussing properties, and the words washed over her head like waves over a beach. She heard but had stopped listening. This was what it was like, she thought, when your world caved in. Even when she had married Jeremy, she had not felt quite so desolate. Perhaps at the back of her mind there had always burnt a tiny, flickering flame of hope that

one day things would work out. Now the hope had been
extinguished, and she felt as if she were staring into one
long, dark tunnel which stretched into eternity.

She resurfaced when the doorbell went, and her mother
left in a cloud of hugs and promises to call every night.

Then there were just the two of them. She couldn't
begin to think how they could break the silence between
them, but when Lorenzo did speak, it was in a cool,
controlled voice.

He politely asked her what she intended doing about
her own house, and she replied, with equal politeness,
that she would be selling it.

'It's much too big for one,' she said, looking more or
less through him. 'Besides, it was never much to my
liking.'

The market was not good for selling houses. They discussed this for some time, and when that conversation
tapered off Lorenzo told her what he thought of property
in Chicago.

Was this how he imagined them together? she wondered. A life of being eaten away by love, love which
she would have to keep to herself, while he treated their
relationship as an ownership long awaited, a passion for
revenge at last fulfilled? While his blonde amused him
on the side?

They ate in silence but then, as Isobel laid down her
knife and fork, she said, without looking at him, 'I just
can't do it, Lorenzo. I just can't marry you, I couldn't
bear it.'

He sat back and regarded her calmly, folding his arms.

'Why not, Isobel?'

'I can't marry you when there's nothing between us
now but dislike. I would keep remembering the
good times.'

There was a dull flush on his cheeks. 'Why would you do that? I doubt you remembered them for four years when you were with Jeremy.' His mouth twisted and she flinched.

'You'll never let me forget that, will you?' she asked, and his face hardened.

'What you did to me stayed with me for four years. Why should I let you forget anything?' He banged his fist on the table, then raked his fingers through his hair.

'It would be better if you left, if you carried on with your life in America...'

'Don't tell me what I would be better off doing!' He stood up, his eyes angry, then he stalked off and she followed towards the sitting-room, just as the telephone began to ring.

She spoke briefly, but her heart had turned to ice and she felt quite sick and disorientated. 'It's for you,' she said, her hand rigid as she held out the telephone.

'For me?'

'Yes. Jessica Tate. Apparently she phoned through to the Edwardian and was given your number here. Lucky we aren't ex-directory, wouldn't you say?'

I hate you, she thought as she handed him the telephone and heard his husky, velvety voice address the woman on the other end. I hate you for coming back into my life.

CHAPTER EIGHT

ISOBEL stood inside the beamed Tudor house and decided that, like it or not, this was going to be the house. The house which she had been looking for for the past two weeks. The house which would put an end to Lorenzo's presence under her mother's roof.

She looked around her and thought that it was in a somewhat sad state of disrepair, but there was nothing that could not be mended with enough money, and there was no shortage of that.

Mr Evans had lent her the keys so that she could look around herself, and had devoutly informed her that the only reason that it was still on the market was because most people were unwilling to move into a place which needed some work done on it.

'Some work', she quickly realised as she went from room to room, was estate agent's jargon for 'total overhaul', but it was, she had to admit, a delightful property. Large, without being sprawling, with the required picture-book garden, or at least the makings of one once the general wilderness had been cleared.

The owners, he had told her, shaking his head ruefully, had sadly been forced to sell.

'Family problems,' he had said enigmatically, and she nodded. She could sympathise with family problems. She had a very active ongoing one at the moment.

The past fortnight had been miserable. True, she had not seen a great deal of Lorenzo, but his presence had invaded every nook and cranny of the house. Every waking moment had been spent in a state of nervous tension in case he walked into the room, or worse in case she found herself alone in a room with him and had to make polite conversation.

What were his plans now? There had been no more dark threats about marriage, no more harsh demands to be told the reasons for her marriage, but the silence still unsettled her. Had the appearance of his lover made him reconsider his twisted desires for revenge? He had said nothing further after her insistence that she could never marry him, and she suspected that the quiet desperation of her words had done what no heated outburst in the past had achieved, but he didn't say and she didn't ask.

Lorenzo, when he addressed her, did so with the distance of a stranger, and that cut her to the quick. When he had returned he had made his hatred of her quite clear, but at least, in retrospect, it had indicated feeling of sorts. Now there was cool indifference in his voice when he spoke to her.

She walked up the narrow staircase into the myriad bedrooms with their curious, charming eccentricities and stood for a while at the window of the master bedroom, gazing down at the untamed garden below.

She didn't want to think about Jessica Tate but she couldn't help herself.

Two days after her telephone call, she had arrived. Lorenzo had rented a flat for her on the outskirts of the town, but that had scarcely minimised her uninvited appearances at the house.

She was keeping tabs on him. Isobel had recognised that from the moment she had first walked through the front door, full of shallow charm and even more full of significant little gestures towards Lorenzo, making it quite clear that he was *her* property.

Isobel looked around the room and thought that the house was perfect, in fact it was so perfect it was almost a shame to hand it over lock, stock and barrel to Lorenzo, but she was quietly going crazy with him living under the same roof.

She inspected the rest of the bedrooms at a leisurely pace. The windows all needed work doing on them, the walls were in dire need of repainting, and the carpets looked as though their sell-by date had been decades back.

She began drifting back downstairs and told herself sternly to concentrate on the house and not on Jessica, but she couldn't. Was that why Lorenzo had been around so little? Because all his spare time was eaten up sleeping with his mistress? She tried hard not to care but the question plagued her. She had found herself thinking about them together, making love, at the most inappropriate moments. At the frozen foods section in the supermarket, in the middle of conversations with people, and of course late at night, when everything seemed so much worse anyway.

Jessica Tate, viewed objectively, unemotionally, was the sort of woman guaranteed to put off most of her female counterparts. She exuded an aura of intelligent competence which, in combination with her impeccably groomed blonde good looks, induced an immediate re-action of wariness.

She was tall, though not as tall as Isobel, with closely cropped blonde hair and cool blue eyes which assessed everyone and everything. They had instantly assessed *her* and had seemed to decide, after some internal debate, that Isobel was not an ongoing threat.

You may have looks, those hard eyes said, but as far as intelligence goes, you're nothing compared to me.

Consequently the majority of her small talk, when it was directed towards Isobel, had been condescending and Isobel, with barely forced politeness, saw no reason to try and justify her existence in the eyes of a woman who looked as though she didn't make a habit of smiling.

'It's such a *responsibility* being promoted over and over again,' she had asserted on her first visit to the house, over a cup of tea, and scones which she had assumed were home-made, because, she had implied, what else did someone like Isobel have to do with her time when her little chores at the local surgery were finished? 'Sometimes I sit back and think how *wonderful*——' pointed cat-like look at Isobel '—it would be to throw it all in and do something completely undemanding for a few years.'

Isobel had smiled politely and murmured something innocuous, while thinking that she had never seen anyone express an observation with such insincerity in her life before.

But Lorenzo had obviously missed it because he had looked at the blonde with a veiled smile of amused indulgence.

'Although,' Jessica had resumed, crinkling her nose at Lorenzo flirtatiously, 'I would probably die of boredom after a couple of weeks.'

She was fond of making little self-disparaging comments, Isobel soon realised, which she would then quickly nullify by building herself up with a practised, bewildered shake of her head. A sort of 'I don't *want* to be terribly popular' approach. 'It's not as though I try very hard, but I just can't seem to stop everyone responding to me!'

You're just being catty, Isobel told herself now. She strolled into the kitchen and was confronted by another sad state of affairs. The dimensions were lovely, but everything had been left to rot and there were huge gaps where the paint had flaked off and something which suspiciously reminded her of mould was creeping into the edges of the walls.

Jessica was coming over to dinner later that evening. Isobel gazed at the creeping mould and thought how much she hated the prospect of having to endure at least three hours in the company of a woman who did everything possible, in the least direct way, to make her feel inadequate and unfulfilled.

'This is such a quaint little village,' she had told Isobel at a later date. 'I guess it's all gossip and wagging of tongues around here? Just like in your lovely British movies?' Her eyes, patronising, had said, What a dull life you lead, gossiping from dawn till dusk. Look at me, I'm smart and successful. Any wonder Lorenzo thinks I'm the bee's knees?

She made damn sure that finance was discussed in the most complex terms possible, and her eyes, sliding along to Isobel, would reinforce that unspoken message which she had been communicating from the very first moment she had arrived.

There was a loud bang on the front door, which knocked the thoughts out of her head, and Isobel sprinted across to open it. It could only be Mr Evans, probably here to give her a little pep talk on the charming possibilities of the cottage. He would point out the original beams, the lovely view from every window, the marvellous fireplace in the sitting-room, and he would disarmingly play down the immense amount of money needed to bring it all up to any reasonable living standard.

She opened the door with a dry smile, and was stunned to discover that the amiable Mr Evans was nowhere on the horizon.

Lorenzo looked down at her, his eyes glittering in the fast-gathering gloom of twilight.

'Oh, hello,' Isobel said, as her nervous system shifted up a couple of notches. He must have come straight from work. He was still wearing his suit, and the long, black coat which made him look like a highwayman. 'What are you doing here?' she asked automatically, and he raised his black eyebrows in a question.

'I'll give you three guesses, shall I?' he asked drily. 'Is there any chance you might stop barricading the door so that I can come in?'

Isobel stood aside and watched as he walked past her and into the centre of the hall.

It was, she thought with a little spurt of dread, the first time in two weeks that they had been alone together. Really alone. Not merely positioned in the same room, more often than not with Jessica providing a third party.

He looked around him, and she said, closing the door, 'How did you know where to find me?'

His eyes lazily made their way back to her face. 'Evans told me,' he answered, sticking his hands into the pockets of his coat. She didn't blame him either. It was freezing in the house. She herself was amply covered in jeans, vest, jumper, and her father's old Barbour which she had always loved so much. She could still feel the cold, though.

'He thought, strange though it might seem, that I would be interested in joining you here to see what I thought of the place.'

The light shone bleakly down from the naked light bulb, and it picked up all the sharp angles of his face, the intense blackness of his hair, the clever, glittering eyes. Funny how intimidating a man could be without really having to try.

'Well, I've already had a look around,' Isobel said weakly, and he moved towards her. Nothing threatening, but she still took a step backwards, and then gritted her teeth together in irritation at behaving so childishly.

'Good,' Lorenzo drawled, 'so you'll be able to give me a comprehensive guided tour.'

'Of course.' She headed off towards the staircase, very businesslike, and he followed her, his footsteps stealthy for a man of his size.

She got the vague feeling that something had changed in him, that he had reached some sort of decision, although it might well have been in her imagination.

She began pointing out the various features, which she was certain he could see for himself without having to have her play the tour guide.

'Only two bathrooms, I'm afraid,' she said, then added, because she couldn't resist, 'I don't know what your penthouse suite was like in Chicago, but houses of this age don't run to massive *en suite* dressing-rooms with separte inbuilt wardrobes for suits and shirts.'

'Don't they?' he asked softly, from nearer behind her than she had thought. 'You do surprise me with that little gem of insight.'

'Bathroom,' she said, pushing open a door. 'A bit small, I'm sure you'll find.'

'A little decrepit, at any rate,' he commented, walking in and surveying the walls and ceiling thoughtfully.

She followed the line of his gaze and murmured wryly, 'Matches the rest of the house. Apparently the owners were forced to sell. I suspect that, long before that, they'd run out of money. Or at least they'd decided to stop spending what they did have on their house.'

'Shame.'

They did the rounds of the bedrooms, which followed no formal logical pattern and required the occasional dodging under low, beamed door-frames, and after they had completed a similar circuit of downstairs, he turned to her and asked, casually, 'What do you think of it?'

They were in the sitting-room. It was the only room where any form of active residence could be glimpsed. This was in the form of yellowed net curtains precariously hanging from the windows. They were old and faded enough not to warrant their removal. Cobwebs clung to the walls and the dust which covered every square inch would have set Cinderella back by a good few weeks.

'I rather like it,' she admitted a little defiantly. 'It has atmosphere.'

'It's run down.'

'With a little restoration, it could be beautiful.'

'It would give any chartered surveyor an apoplectic fit.'

'A little painting,' she said with great understatement, glancing around her and using her imagination to restore it to its full potential. 'Some lovely old furniture, bowls of flowers.'

'Massive structural work...'

'The odd bit of structural work...'

He threw back his head and laughed at that, and she grinned at him reluctantly.

'Are you sure that you're not being persuasive because you want me out of your mother's house?' he asked.

'Of course not!'

'Or because you're secretly in Mr Evan's employ?'

'Heaven forbid! Although he *did* know my father...'

'Then why don't you sit down and tell me why you think I should invest my money in this place.'

Isobel looked around her and said matter-of-factly, 'My eyes must be failing. I can't see any chairs.'

'Who needs chairs?' He took off his coat and laid it by the wall and pointed her towards it in a sweeping gesture, with a theatrical little bow, and she laughed, relaxing her guard. He was being friendly, she realised, and some part of her felt vaguely upset at that, though she didn't know why.

'Well,' she began, sitting down and feeling a shiver of apprehension as he lowered his lean frame next to her, 'I doubt you'll find anything as charming as this anywhere around here. It's a damned sight nicer than any of the properties I've looked around, and I've seen a lot. OK, so you'll need to have some work done on it, but what else can you expect of an old property that's had no money spent on it in years?'

'What indeed?' he murmured, and she felt that shiver of apprehension again.

'There are six bedrooms.'

'More than enough to entertain the occasional overnight guest,' he agreed, looking at her.

'And the garden would be a challenge for your mother.'

'Why didn't you and Jeremy ever have children?' he asked softly, out of the blue, and she sighed wryly, looking at him.

'I thought you'd given up asking those questions.'

'Because you refuse to give answers?'

'You'll have to pull out the kitchen and start from scratch. That room looks as though it might pose a serious health hazard.'

'You have nothing to fear from me, Isobel,' he murmured. 'I admit that when I first returned here I would have liked nothing better than to have made you suffer the way you once made me suffer, but you were right. All that is behind us now. I've thought about what you said, about not being able to marry me, and you're right.

Revenge can be taken so far and then beyond that it becomes insanity. So what I want to say is that you're free. I'll buy your father's company, no strings attached. We can never be friends, but it's time for the past to be put to rest.'

That, she knew, should have sent her spirits soaring. Instead she felt a blinding sense of loss, the loss of the man whom she still loved to distraction, but who had now put her behind him, an unfortunate episode in his past which had once hurt but no longer did.

She knew as well, that she could tell him why she had married Jeremy, and she would have nothing to fear. He would not use the knowledge over her and, deep down, she had known that he never would.

But she would never tell him. She realised that now, with great sadness, because how could she explain her most intimate and private agony to a man who didn't love her? Her secret, like it or not, was now hers forever. There was no chance that she would ever share it with anyone because she would only share it with a man she loved, a man who returned her love, and that was the one thing Lorenzo would never do.

Sitting here, with his legs so close to hers, his body emanating warmth, reminding her of past things, she just felt ready to cry.

'In the end, he won, didn't he?' Lorenzo asked. 'He drove us apart four years ago because he hated me. The fact that you were something to pin on his jacket, something to adorn his arm, was an added bonus.'

She frowned, puzzled. 'Lorenzo, you've said that once before. That he hated you. But he had no reason to...'

'Oh, but he had.' Lorenzo took her face between his hands. 'I discovered something about him, quite by accident, you see.'

She was completely lost now. What on earth was he talking about?

'Do you remember my mother used to clean for his? A long, long time ago?'

Isobel nodded. There was a stillness in the air that made her hairs stand on end.

'One day, Emily Baker was there. She had had a little too much to drink and she was in a maudlin mood. Heaven knows, she always tended to be neurotic, from what I had seen.' He paused and looked at her, and in the half-shadows his pale eyes seemed black and bottomless. 'My mother was about to leave but she was worried about Jeremy's mother. Knowing Mama, she probably said something along the lines of, Is anything the matter? Anyway, out it all came. She began pouring her heart out. Guilt over something she had done years back.' He looked at her.

'Are you telling me that her husband was not Jeremy's father?'

'Apparently he couldn't have children.' Lorenzo sighed. 'Isn't it ironic the amount of people who seem to spawn children like rabbits, when there are others, worthwhile good men, who can't? Anyway, she had a brief affair and hence the birth nine months later of Jeremy. I suppose it was a confession that would have sunk into oblivion. Certainly Mama would never have said anything further about it, and I can't imagine that Emily would have considered it dinner-party conversation. But Jeremy walked in on the little scene. He made ugly, derogatory comments to his mother. He was shocked. She had never mentioned a word of it before.'

'But what did that have to do with you?'

'He assumed that my mother had told me, which of course she had, in the mistaken illusion that I could talk to him, lend a sympathetic ear. But Jeremy had never been one for the sympathetic ear. Months later, when it had been fermenting away inside him, he accused me of acting as though I was superior to him. He threw his parentage into my face, said that I'd probably been sniggering about it behind his back, and I did the worst possible thing. I laughed. Laughed that he could have been so off-target. But he misinterpreted my reaction, thought I was laughing at him, and he hit the roof. He said that one day he'd get even, and naturally I didn't pay a blind bit of notice to that. But he did, didn't he, Isobel?'

She nodded, digesting what he had just told her. It accounted for a lot of things, for Jeremy's sarcasm whenever Lorenzo's name was mentioned, and his recklessness, his dependence on drink. Did it all stem from that? He had never, ever discussed his parents with her and she had never had a clue about Emily Baker, but why should she? To outside eyes his parents were a happy couple, and chances were that her single sin had been a peccadillo born of depression, something that passed in time.

It had begun to rain. Autumn seemed to have been drenched with rain. She heard the steady drumming of raindrops against the window-pane.

'I suppose,' she said, 'we ought to be getting back.'

He looked at her, hesitating, then he said, standing up, 'I suppose so.'

'Isn't this awful weather?' she murmured as they walked towards the front door.

'Worse than Chicago,' he agreed, 'and that was bad enough. The winters were hard, but the summers were good. Seasons behaved themselves the way they ought to.'

She smiled and automatically raised her eyes to his, and for a split-second she thought that he was going to

kiss her. But he didn't. He said slowly, 'I think I might
return to Italy, make my base there.'

'Driven away by the constant rain?' she murmured
lightly, but her heart clenched tightly inside her. 'Is this
your way of telling me that my efforts in finding you
the perfect house have been for nothing?'

'Oh, I don't know,' he shrugged. 'I could always buy
this place, and keep it for the times I return here. I shall
have to oversee the company so I'll be back and forth,
I should imagine. But,' he added, 'we need never cross
paths again.'

Why did that hurt so much? She should be singing
for joy. She opened the door, letting in a spray of rain,
and ran towards her mother's car. Part of her knew that
never setting eyes on him again was the best possible
thing for her mental health, but there was another part,
the same little desperate part that had been with her for
the past four years, telling her that to glimpse him fleet-
ingly was better than nothing.

She fumbled with the lock while he watched calmly,
getting wet, and when she had settled into the driver's
seat he went across to his own car, letting her leave first,
then following slowly behind her.

Jessica was already there by the time they made it back
to the house. There and looking none too pleased as
they made their wet entry into the hall.

'Where have you been?' she asked solicitously. 'You're
soaked.' She fussed around Lorenzo, who shrugged off
her attentiveness with irritation.

'We were looking at a house,' he said briefly.

'Oh, yes.' She glanced at Isobel, eyes hard. 'I forgot
that you were playing the estate agent. However do you
find the time? I do wish I could have had someone
running around to find my apartment in Chicago! It

would have saved me a lot of valuable time. And was it a success?'

'We think so,' Lorenzo said, and Jessica's eyes hardened a little bit more. She didn't like the 'we' bit, it was just a mite too familiar for her, even though Isobel could have told her that she had nothing to fear on that score.

She left her in the hall, still unsuccessfully clucking around Lorenzo, and removed herself to her bedroom, where she had an overlong bath and, after eyeing her wardrobe critically, slipped on an ivory-coloured calf-length skirt and a short-sleeved, figure-hugging jumper in the same colour. The reflection staring back at her was tremendously beautiful. Isobel looked at herself without vanity and wondered why people ever imagined that looks brought happiness. In her case, it couldn't have been further from the truth.

Then she sat down on the dressing-table chair and thought about what Lorenzo had told her. Would she have reacted differently to Jeremy if she had known the true facts about him? She thought not. For the first time she contemplated her past calmly, without rancour.

She had been forced into a marriage through circumstances and, even though she had tasted the bitter fruit of unhappiness, she would have done the same thing if she had had to make the choice all over again.

In a way, it had worked to her advantage that she had not loved Jeremy. It had given her a sublime indifference to the rather unpleasant sides of his character, the tendency towards bullying, the mood swings, the bursts of unbearable arrogance. He was like a wilful child, incapable of understanding that the world did not revolve around him.

Would Lorenzo really return to Italy to live? she wondered, playing with the brush on the dressing-table. It was more than likely. Whether he ever really admitted it or not, she knew that she was the reason that he had returned to Yorkshire in the first place, back to the town that he had left behind in bitter anger. He had purged his system of her now. He was free.

Oh, God, she thought desperately, will *I* ever be free? Lorenzo was still the man who held her dreams in the palm of his hand. She could see herself in twenty years' time and she could imagine the whispers of people around her, saying to each other, She was so beautiful once. Why didn't she ever remarry? She'll never catch a man now, of course! Far too old.

There was a knock on the door and she looked up, startled. If I don't watch it, she thought grimly, I shall find myself becoming one of those awful women who live in a world of self-pity and can't see beyond their own miseries.

It was Jessica. That startled Isobel even more. Not once had the other woman ventured up to her bedroom.

'I wanted to have a word with you alone,' Jessica said, looking around her with mild curiosity. She was the sort of woman to whom even the Seven Wonders of the World would afford only mild curiosity. She stood in the centre of the room and folded her arms. 'I wanted to tell you that I've been sacked.' Her eyes narrowed to slits. 'Politely told that my accounting services are no longer required.'

'Really?'

'Please,' she drawled, 'spare me the wide-eyed innocence. We're both women of the world. When I first came here I decided that I wouldn't see you as a threat. Why should I? Sure, you have those looks, but types like you are a dime a dozen. All beauty and no brains. Look at you, stuck in this godforsaken place beyond the back of civilisation! *Not* the sort to appeal to the Lorenzo I knew.'

'Why are you telling me all this?' Isobel asked in a tight voice.

'Because I just want to warn you that you haven't won, even though you may think that you have.' Jessica was looking positively malicious. A little feline smile played on her well-painted lips.

'We really ought to be going downstairs,' Isobel decided.

'Not until I've said what I came to say. I wasted four years on that man. No one, but *no one*, takes Jessica Tate for a ride!'

The vehemence in the voice stunned Isobel back into silence. She could believe that no one had ever taken the great Jessica Tate for a ride. She looked the sort who monopolised taking other people for rides.

'It's hardly my fault that——'

'It damn well is! I don't know what happened between the two of you years ago, but whatever it was, he still wants you.' She spat that out with venom.

Wanted, Isobel thought disjointedly.

'But I haven't invested my time in that man for nothing!' She made it sound like a business venture that had gone wrong. Isobel could imagine her making up a list of the pros and cons of getting involved with him, working out whether he was worth the time and effort.

'I'm sorry,' Isobel said coldly, not feeling in the least sorry, 'if you fell in love with Lorenzo——'

'Fell in love with him?' She laughed acidly. 'I'm not some fifteen-year-old teenager, my dear! He's sexy, though, I'll admit that, but most of all he was a good catch. I suppose you thought that your ship had come in when you discovered that he was going to be in town?'

'Quite the opposite.'

'You British!' she said scathingly. 'Well, your ship may have docked but it's not going to remain too long in port. I'll make damn sure of that.' She smiled again, hugging something to herself, and Isobel looked at her uneasily.

With anyone else she would have admitted that she and Lorenzo had nothing, that any reluctant feeling he had had for her had now been extinguished, but she kept quiet.

But, throughout the evening, her eyes kept flitting back worriedly to Jessica's over-bright face, the over-wide smile.

She announced over dinner in a casual voice that she would be leaving within the week.

'No offence, but I'd be stifled here,' she said in that bursting-with-confidence tone of voice which implied that her departure would leave the community bereft, but what could she do?

Then she proceeded to launch into a monologue on what a valuable asset she was to the world of business.

Isobel remained silent, on edge, barely looking at Lorenzo, who appeared to have switched off from the conversation, wondering when she could make an exit.

She had never thought that hearing him speak to her in those neutral tones, seeing him look at her in that expressionless, courteous way, could have made her heart constrict, but it did. The past was now buried, and his manner towards her now spoke of sublime indifference.

She bleakly switched off from her surroundings too, listening to the thoughts whirling around in her head, while Jessica, who seemed to be burning with inextinguishable sparks of energy, talked about the opportunities waiting for her back in Chicago.

She *had* made a fool of herself, Isobel thought. Or at least she believed so, in rushing out here at Lorenzo's beckoning, and now she was extricating herself as efficiently as she could, so that she could think later that she had been lucky, that she had had a narrow escape.

'Of course, I shall pull strings to make sure that you get a good job,' Lorenzo said when there was a break in the conversation, and Jessica threw him a deadly smile.

'That won't be necessary. I have quite a few valuable contacts of my own.'

He shrugged, and a flash of rage crossed the hard, tight-lipped face.

This was getting distinctly uncomfortable. Isobel stood up, ready to take her leave and extricate herself from the thick, highly-charged atmosphere, but Jessica looked at her with a small smile of pleasure, and said tightly, 'Oh, before you go, Isobel.' It was the first time she had called her by her name, Isobel realised. 'There are just a few little things I feel you ought to see.' She walked across the room and picked up her briefcase which had been lying on the chair by the door.

Isobel hadn't even noticed it.

'What little things?'

'Oh, a few bits and pieces to do with your father's company. I know no deal has been formalised, but I had some spare time last week and I thought I'd mosey along and see what the company accounts looked like. I told them that the deal was more or less wrapped up and of course they believed me. Wonderful, these little hick towns.'

Lorenzo threw her a furious look but she was beyond the reach of his fury now.

'What the hell do you mean by this?' he asked, standing up so that even Jessica cringed back involuntarily. 'Does the word "unethical" mean anything to you?'

'Not always,' she said languidly, bored.

'You had no right,' Isobel said, white-faced, and Jessica laughed.

'Admittedly not,' she said unapologetically, 'but I was curious to see why Lorenzo wanted the company so badly. I wanted to see what hidden reserves there were. If it had been big enough, and if your deal had fallen through, well, let's just say I knew a certain fish that might have wanted the bait, and I knew that you would be in a desperate position with no other buyer in the field.' She was still smiling with a chilling lack of humour. 'And it was certainly an interesting forage, I can tell you!'

She clicked open the briefcase and, after a while, Isobel sat back down. She didn't like the expression of triumph on the other woman's face. It frightened her. Was it really so quiet in the room or was it her imagination? She could hear the sound of the wind outside, and inside the shuffling of the papers on Jessica's lap.

There was a tension about Lorenzo as well. She sneaked a glance at him from under her lashes and wondered what he was thinking.

'For God's sake, Jessica,' he snapped impatiently, 'is all this really necessary at——' he consulted his watch '—quarter past twelve? It's been a long day and I'm not about to stay here discussing business until all hours of the morning.'

'I won't be a minute,' Jessica said, not looking at him. After a while she glanced up with satisfaction and said, 'There. Now——' she looked at them both '—who would like to be the first to peruse these *very* interesting documents?'

She sounded like someone who was about to start an auction going, and was fairly guaranteed an enthusiastic response.

She was holding a small wad of papers in her hand, and all of a sudden, in one sickening moment of realisation, Isobel knew, knew with a sense of building dread what those '*very* interesting documents' were.

She had not found the incriminating evidence among Jeremy's things, had she? But that hadn't worried her. She had assumed that they would turn up sooner or later. After all, she had hardly really searched in depth for them. Too much had been going on for her to devote time to that.

How was she to have known that he hadn't concealed them in the house after all?

'Where,' she asked, white-faced, 'did you find those?'

'Oh, interested suddenly, are you?' Jessica smiled smugly. 'Accountants. You'd be surprised what we find in nooks and crannies. I was rummaging through your late husband's desk drawer, where I had been cheerfully escorted and left on my own, and imagine my amazement when I discovered that it had a false bottom. I thought that sort of thing only happened in movies! Naturally I prised it open.' She was deriving great pleasure from telling them all this.

'What the hell is all this about, Jessica?' Lorenzo asked in a dangerously soft voice.

She didn't answer. She held out the papers and said sweetly, 'Bedtime reading for you.' She stood up and dusted herself down. 'Now, I really must be going.' She turned to Isobel. 'I won't see you again. I'm sure you'll be as sad as I am at the thought of that. Now, I'll leave you two together, shall I? There's a lot, I suspect, that you'll want to discuss.'

With that she left, closing the door behind her, and Isobel stared at Lorenzo with wide eyes. Then she did something she had never done in her life before.

She blacked out.

CHAPTER NINE

WHEN Isobel next opened her eyes, she was on the sofa, lying down. It took her a few seconds to try and work out what she was doing in this peculiar position, then she sat up suddenly, her body tense as she looked at Lorenzo's downbent head.

He was reading the papers, his long fingers flicking through them, re-reading bits, absorbing it all.

In a way it was a relief that everything would now be out in the open, at least between the two of them.

He glanced up at her with expressionless eyes and said in a hard voice, 'Why didn't you tell me?'

Isobel licked her lips. 'How could I?' she asked helplessly, and he flung the papers down on the table and began pacing the room, his movements restless, his hands shoved into his trouser pockets.

She followed him with her eyes, compulsively drinking in his movements, the angry hunch of his powerful shoulders, the tight line of his mouth.

He stopped in front of her and stared down. 'Very easily,' he said coldly, in a voice that made her flinch. 'Try and understand my position...!'

'Your "*position*" was that you allowed yourself to be blackmailed by a man intent on getting what he wanted at all costs!'

'Oh, what's the point?' she muttered, sinking down into the chair. 'What's the point in trying to explain anything to you? You don't want to understand.'

He sat down on the coffee-table in front of her and she reluctantly watched him.

156

'What your father did was not the end of the world,' he said in a tight voice, and her eyes flashed angrily back at him.

'Not the end of the world, no! But if it had ever become public knowledge, my parents' lives would have been destroyed. In a town of this size, where everyone knows everyone else, where my father was a big name, God help him, the publicity would have ruined him.'

'When did Jeremy find out about it?' Lorenzo asked. 'And don't,' he added icily, 'try and walk out on an explanation now. I intend to hear every word of what you've got to say, if I have to nail you to the sofa personally.'

His eyes were full of hatred. The frozen politeness which had been there before had gone.

Isobel sighed and lay back, half closing her eyes.

'He telephoned me one night at university,' she said quietly. 'He always telephoned me. I never told you because I knew you would fly into a blind rage. Jeremy——' she hesitated '—couldn't seem to let me go. He hated the fact that we were going out together. He hated your presence in my life. That night he sounded excited, on a high. He told me that he had found out something, something that could affect me personally. He said that he wanted to come up and see me to discuss it, and naturally I told him to get lost.' She laughed to herself. 'I told him that I . . .' She remembered what she had told him, that she was in love with Lorenzo Cicolla, but for some reason she couldn't bring herself to say that now. 'I told him that I was involved with you and that I didn't want him to contact me again.'

'You damn well should have said something to me about all that!' Lorenzo informed her, with fury in his voice, and she opened her eyes to look him fully in the face.

'It wouldn't have been worth it. Besides, I suppose I felt sorry for Jeremy. We had known each other since our childhood days, and even if he had gone a bit off the rails then there was still enough of a shared past for me to want to try and avoid hurting him. Unnecessarily.'

'So what was his next move?' He stood up and walked across to the bar in the corner of the room and poured himself a drink, offering her one, which she refused. Then he returned to where he had been sitting and swallowed the lot in one mouthful.

'He wrote to me. He told me that he had come across some papers, that he had evidence that my father had been ...' Her voice faltered at this point. 'If it had been a question of another woman, I would have been concerned, but that would have been different. My mother would have been dreadfully hurt, and so would I, but people would have forgotten about it within weeks. But this was different.'

'This brought the whole question of his trustworthiness into dispute,' Lorenzo filled in for her and she nodded miserably.

'He was a pillar of the community. If it were ever known that he had been embezzling money...' There, it was out, the secret that she had clung on to for so long that it had almost become a part of her, like a dark tumour.

The silence in the room pounded in her ears and she couldn't meet Lorenzo's eyes.

'Jeremy had been going through old files. Files which should have been consigned to the incinerator, but for some reason had not been. Well, you know how Dad was a compulsive jotter. He used to say that he thought better when he could see it in front of him, so he'd jot down things. In this file were jottings. Pages of them.

Plans meticulously worked out to defraud the company. Jeremy told me that he knew how it had been done.'

'I suppose he did it between audits?'

'So I gather,' Isobel muttered, eyes still down. 'I read all the bits of paper over and over, trying to convince myself that I was mistaken, but it appeared that Dad had set up bogus companies, something like that anyway, with money being paid to non-existent suppliers.'

'You saw the accounts?'

Isobel shook her head. 'Destroyed, I suppose, but the jottings were enough. They were Dad's handwriting. On that alone... It was enough.'

'Did you confront him with it?'

'Of course not!' She looked at him, horrified at that. 'I loved my father. I loved him whatever he had done. Jeremy had the information at hand to destroy him if he wanted and I couldn't let him do that.'

'So you agreed to whatever he wanted.' It was a cold statement of fact and she winced.

'I had no choice. He was obsessed with me, and with taking me away from you, although until you told me about his background, I never fully understood the reason why.'

'So little Isobel buckled down under pressure and played the dutiful wife.' The contempt in his voice made her flush with sudden anger.

'And what,' she suggested fiercely, 'would you have suggested I did? What would you have done if I had come running to you with the story? I know what you would have done! You would have stormed up here to see Jeremy and you would have tried to thrash him into submission!'

'Are you telling me that he wouldn't have deserved it?'

'I'm telling you that it would have had as much success as plugging a dam with a toothpick! He was always prone to violent tempers, you know that! If you had confronted him, he would have done the first thing that came into his head! He would have announced his little gem of information loud and clear, to all and sundry!'

'And what else did he blackmail you into doing, Isobel?' He leaned towards her, his face dark and savage. 'Did he blackmail you into making love to him whenever he wanted you?'

She gripped the cushions on the sofa. 'Does it matter?'

'Tell me, damn you!' He dragged her head up so that she had to meet his glittering eyes.

'I...' She took a deep breath, terrified at what she saw on Lorenzo's face. 'I couldn't. He tried, but it was hopeless. I think he must have found...fulfilment with other women. He went on business trips quite a bit.' Her voice had sunk to a whisper. 'He was content to have me as a decoration, to see the envy in his friends' eyes occasionally, to know, I guess, that he had killed whatever the two of us had had.'

'Why didn't you tell me all this when I returned here?' he asked, and his voice was like a whiplash. He wasn't about to forgive her. He would never forgive her. His own impulses were not to submission. He would never really understand, she thought despairingly.

'How could I?'

'Jeremy was dead. He had no hold over you any longer.' He said that flatly, as though it made all the sense in the world, as though her continuing silence had been nothing more than stupidity on her part.

'So what...?' she asked bitterly. 'So after four years I should see you staring at me, an opponent, and confess all?' She laughed harshly, laughter on the verge of tears. 'You hate me, Lorenzo. You made that clear the minute you returned. And yet you're telling me now that I should have trusted you?'

'Did you think that I might use the information to get back at you, Isobel?' His mouth curled into a sneer. 'You insult me by implying that I would have done any such thing!'

'I . . . I don't suppose I thought that you would. No, deep down I knew that you wouldn't, but I wasn't about to take the chance. My mother is ill, vulnerable . . .' She saw another flash of immense fury in his eyes and shivered. 'Besides,' she continued defiantly, 'when you returned here, you returned a stranger. You weren't the same person I knew all those years ago! I *couldn't* confide in you. I no longer *knew* you. You talked of revenge, hatred . . .'

'What it boils down to, Isobel,' he grated harshly, 'is that you didn't trust me. You never trusted me.'

'That's not true!' She leaned towards him but there was no softening in his face.

'No?' he mocked. 'I could have talked to him, made him see sense.'

'He would never have seen sense. I should know, I lived with him for four years.' Her eyes clouded over with memory. 'Jeremy never really grew up. Oh, he acted the part of the adult, he could make witty conversation when it was necessary, but deep down he was like a child. If things didn't go his way, he could throw the most frightful tempers. I learned to get out of his way. I learned to keep myself apart, detached.'

'You learned to sacrifice your life. You walked out on me.'

She hung her head, not knowing what to say, tired of defending herself.

'Don't tell me that you spent all that time pining,' she muttered unsteadily. 'I should think that you quickly recovered from the body-blow to your pride. After all, you showed up here with Jessica Tate in your wake, making it obvious what your relationship with her was! Where did she fall in the queue of women, Lorenzo?'

They stared at one another, and in the semi-darkness of the room her heart skipped a beat.

She stood up. Her legs felt wobbly.

'Not so fast,' he murmured from next to her. 'When you walked out on me, you left unfinished business behind.'

'What are you talking about?'

'I'm talking about this.' He reached out and pulled her towards him, and his mouth met hers with the force of anger and desire.

Isobel groaned and struggled against him, but he wasn't letting go and, under the force of his embrace, she found her lips parting, her tongue flicking with excitement against his.

She knew what he was doing. Emotionally he had expunged her from his system, but against his will there was still desire there, and desire was what he now aimed to clear once and for all.

There was an urgency in him, emanating from his body, and with a gesture of defeat she wound her arms around his neck and surrendered to her impulses.

Why fight it? she thought to herself. If this was to be their bitter parting, then why not yield? Hadn't she fantasised about this for a long time? His image had followed her every day and every night for as long as she could remember.

He lifted her up in one swift movement and carried her across to the rug in front of the fireplace. She didn't have to see his face to know that every touch was fired by a sort of savage passion. But there was a savage passion burning inside her as well, only she knew that this would not expunge him from her system because emotionally he was still there and always would be.

He unbuttoned his shirt unsteadily, tugging it out of his trousers, then lay down next to her, holding her face between his fingers and kissing her until she gasped for breath.

'I can't stand the thought that he touched you, Isobel,' he muttered against her neck, his voice rough, and there was enough possessive passion there to send her spirits soaring, but not for long. She had hurt him, but not fatally, not as he had hurt her in the end.

His hand slipped beneath the cotton jumper and he massage her breast through the lacy bra until she writhed with pleasure.

With shaking fingers she unhooked it from the front, pulling it aside so that there was now no barrier between his fingers and the soft swell of her breasts, their nipples swollen with aching anticipation.

He groaned and pushed up the jumper, seeking her breasts like an infant searching for its source of food. She watched his dark head as his mouth fastened to her nipple and he pulled at it, drawing it into his mouth.

She knew that she would gain so much and lose so much by making love to him, but she couldn't begin to reason it out. She just knew that it was inevitable.

As he suckled on her breast, he unzipped her skirt, pulling her free of it and tossing it on one of the chairs, then her lacy underwear followed so that she was lying against him, naked.

He half raised himself to look at her, and she watched him with a mixture of sadness and pleasure. There was no concealing the primeval want in his eyes.

He stood up, still staring at her, his breath coming and going as quickly as hers was, and she looked as he undressed, taking in every smooth, hard line of his body as though she had never seen it before.

He stooped beside her, moulding her with his hands, her breasts, her stomach, her waist, then he bent and kissed her thighs, working up until his mouth had found her most private places, sending her into a vortex of raging desire. She parted her legs to accommodate the flicking of his tongue as he explored every inch of her, and when she thought that she could no longer contain the dam of excitement waiting to burst, he eased himself on her and buried his face against her neck.

She could hear him muttering her name over and over again. There was no tenderness there though.

'I don't want to feel this way about you,' he muttered unsteadily, and he looked at her with darkening eyes. 'This passion...'

And I don't want to feel this way about *you*, Lorenzo Cicolla, she told herself. I don't want to feel this overwhelming love, to know that I shall never be able to escape. If only all she felt for him was passion. Passion could be sated. It was a monster that could evaporate once it had been fed to its satisfaction, but love was something else entirely. Love ate away at you and then, when you thought that there was nothing left, it started all over again.

He cupped her neck with his hand as his mouth descended over hers. He thrust into her, his movements slow to start with, then quickening until they found a rhythm of their own and their bodies were joined in unison.

Isobel placed her hands in the small of his back and flung her head backwards as the fire that had been building in her reached its apex, filling her entire being, taking her into another orbit, at least for a while.

She was still trembling when he lay down beside her with his hand behind his head.

There had always been things to say, long ago when they were lovers. Now she listened to the silence, and knew that this would be the last time that she would ever feel that glorious body next to hers.

What was going through his head? Had he been released by their lovemaking?

He turned to her and said in a toneless voice, 'I think it's time for me to go.'

He might as well have told her that he thought it was time for him to leave planet Earth and set up camp on the moon. She could feel the tears pricking the back of her eyes and she didn't dare to look at him because that would have been courting disaster.

In all their discussions about Jeremy, he had never once mentioned feelings, he had never once hinted that he might have felt anything for her beyond all those emotions generated by lost pride. At least she had spared herself the final humiliation of having him know how much she still loved him and always had.

'I'll pack my clothes. I can be out of here within an hour.'

'Yes.' She stood up, woodenly, and began putting on her clothes. She hadn't even thought about contraception, but she knew, with a strange sense of disappointment, that she was not in a fertile period. There wasn't even a chance that this would have led to a baby.

He dressed in silence, then they faced each other across the room.

'Will you make my apologies to your mother when she returns for not staying on?' he asked.

'Yes, I will,' she said with the same feeling of unreality eating away inside her. 'Where will you go?'

'To London for a few days, then I shall fly to Italy. You'll find another buyer for your father's company. Let Clark advise you. My days here are finished.'

Now that there was such a sense of finality between them, she had a compulsive need to keep the conversation going. Whereas before she had been too full of nervous awareness of him to be in the same room, now she would have kept him here as long as she could because she knew that this was the end of the line.

'What will you do about the cottage?' she asked, and he shrugged, moving towards the door.

'There would be no point,' he murmured. 'If and when I do come over here, I can always stay at the hotel.'

'The Edwardian?'

They smiled at each other and she felt a dart of pain.

'It is a bit grim,' he said, 'isn't it? Perhaps things there might improve.' He began walking up the stairs. It was quite black here and her eyes had to adjust to the dark shape ahead of her. At the top he turned to her and said softly, 'Goodbye, Isobel.'

She couldn't see his face. It was just too dark, and she was glad that he could not see hers.

'Goodbye, Lorenzo,' she said, hoping that her voice would see her through and not crack up in mid-sentence. 'And good luck.'

He nodded slightly and then turned away, his footsteps soft and stealthy on the carpet.

Isobel went to her room and sat on her bed with the lights switched off. She felt completely drained. After some time she heard him walk past quietly, and she had to imagine the rest. The soft click of the front door closing behind him, the throb of the engine as he started the car, the headlights beaming as he drove away. Out of this small town that had been responsible for so much, and out of her life.

*   *   *

The following day she felt like someone recovering from a state of shock.

'But *why* did he have to leave at such an extraordinary hour?' her mother asked when she telephoned later that day. 'Did he have a call? Is his mother ill?'

'There were a few problems that needed sorting out straight away,' Isobel replied. 'He felt that he had to go immediately.'

'Yes, I'm sure Lorenzo would have remained unless it was important,' Mrs Chandler said, ever ready to give people the benefit of the doubt. 'You'll miss him, Isobel, I know.'

She couldn't face an outright lie to counteract that one so she held her tongue and stared at the wall in front of her.

'He'll be back,' Mrs Chandler said gently.

'No. He won't.'

'My dear, if you still love him, why did you ever marry Jeremy?'

Isobel's eyes widened in surprise. 'B-Because...' she stammered, 'because it seemed like the right thing to do at the time.'

'We all make mistakes,' her mother sighed from miles away, not pressing the point. 'But Lorenzo will come back, I'm sure of it.'

When hell freezes over, Isobel thought, when the cow jumps over the moon and the dish runs away with the spoon. It was pointless dwelling on it and, when she replaced the receiver, she decided that the only thing to do would be to carry on, to smile and smile and smile for the outside world. She had had enough experience of that.

In fact, she spent the next two days smiling. It certainly convinced the patients that she was in a very good mood indeed, which was something, but the minute she was alone the mask fell away and she found herself contemplating, without any need to disguise it, the long, dark tunnel ahead of her. A thousand pages of a thousand calendars turning over, as the months grew into years and the bleakness in her heart set ever harder by the day.

What had happened to the golden girl who had it all? she wondered. It seemed strange that everything could slip away so completely, like sand between open fingers. One minute the future was in front of her, promising everything, and the next she was confined to a prison, without hope of remission.

By the Friday she felt that she was going out of her mind, so on the spur of the moment she decided to get in touch with Abigail. Abigail could always be relied upon to bring her back down to earth. For some reason, and although she was very close to her mother, she couldn't face talking to her about what had happened. For a start there would be too many bits and pieces that would have to be left out, and there wasn't much chance that she would be able to get through an edited explanation without her mother becoming increasingly suspicious along the way.

The only problem with Abigail was, of course, her schedule. In a fairly nomadic profession, her bases tended to jump from one part of the country to the other, when she *was* in the country at all.

Isobel wrinkled her brow and tried to remember what her friend had told her about her jobs. Where was she now? London? Manchester? Birmingham? She had been doing something, Isobel was sure, at the Alexandra Theatre in Birmingham, but was that now finished?

She dialled her London number. It rang three times, and then on came the chatty, pre-recorded voice of Abigail, informing her that she wasn't available at the moment, but would get back to the caller 'with the speed of light'. The message breathed sincerity, and Isobel half smiled, knowing that her friend only ever got back to a few of her callers, and rarely at the speed of light.

She was mistaken, though. The telephone rang ten minutes later and Abigail said breathlessly down the line, 'I *was* in, Izzy, but I couldn't be bothered to get to the phone.' There was a massive, uninterrupted yawn down the line and Isobel said drily,

'Too much sleep is bad for you.'

'Try telling that to my nervous system,' Abigail said. 'You never phone me, Isobel, which is why—and, please, there's no need to be grateful—I'm phoning you back. What's the matter?'

Isobel sat down. In this huge, empty house, she could talk unhindered for as long as she wanted, and she really wanted to, to pour it all out, but naturally she now found that she couldn't.

'I just thought I'd find out how you were,' she said, postponing the confession.

'Thriving, now that you ask. I'm doing an absolutely marvellous play at the moment here. Not too strenuous, but with some nice, witty dialogue. It's a bit of much-needed light relief before I vanish off to distant shores. New York, to be precise.'

'Oh, what a hard life you lead,' Isobel said jokingly. 'London, New York. Next you'll be telling me that you're honing up on your Far Eastern dialects and will be flying out to Tokyo to dazzle them with your talents.' She laughed, but her fingers played compulsively with the telephone cord.

Abigail must have detected the slight nervous edge to her voice because she said seriously, 'Whatever is wrong, Izzy? I don't have to see you to know that you're not exactly on top of the world. Is it your mother? She's all right, isn't she?'

'It's me, Abby,' Isobel said flatly. 'I have no one else to turn to.' Damn, she was beginning to feel tearful. She took a deep breath and began telling her friend about Lorenzo. Really, she had meant to keep it brief. Who liked being overdosed on someone else's problems? Even a good friend's? But the more she spoke, the more she found that she had to say. It surprised her how much she had taken in of him—had she really noticed him in such agonising detail?

She never mentioned a word about Jeremy, or the reason that she had married him, but she talked and talked and talked. At the end of which, Abigail said, with her usual forthrightness, 'You're a mess.'

'Is that any way to cheer a friend up?' Isobel asked shakily. The tears which had been threatening for the past ten minutes dripped silently down her cheek and she wiped them away with the back of her hand.

'Of course, you'll have to come up here.'

'I can't.'

'Don't be ridiculous. Of course you can and of course you will. No ifs and buts. You can travel up tomorrow morning and spend the weekend with me. I'll get you a ticket to my play, you lucky, *lucky* girl.' Which had the desired effect of making Isobel smile. 'I shan't be at my flat in the morning, so you'll have to make your own way there, but you still have the spare key, don't you? Yes, I can tell you're nodding. Make your way to my flat, help yourself to my food, which won't be very appetising because I'm on a new and improved diet which, as usual, doesn't appear to be working, and then go shopping. That's an order. *Go shopping*. Buy something wonderful to wear to the theatre. It's the last night that the play's on and there will be all sorts of semi-famous faces attending. The really famous ones were there on first night, I'm afraid. We'll have a late supper when the play's finished and the applause has died down. Read my lips, Isobel: You are going to have a stupendous time!'

So at three-thirty the following afternoon, she found herself walking along Bond Street with a cold sun putting in a rare appearance to remind the country at large that it did exist, and browsing for the mandatory outfit for An Evening at the Theatre.

It was quite a few months since she had been to London. She was a country girl at heart and usually found London very claustrophobic, but right now it was wonderful. It just felt good to be somewhere different, and even if thoughts of Lorenzo continued to buzz through her head like a swarm of bees, some of her depression was lifting.

She found herself a glamorous long-sleeved dress in fine, bright green wool and was blushingly flattered when the salesperson asked her whether she was a model. Then she bought some costume jewellery, some shoes, and returned to Abigail's flat at six-thirty, far more heartened than when she had set out on the train down several hours back.

Maybe, she thought as she dressed carefully for the evening, she and her mother could spend an indefinite amount of time travelling. Maybe several years of travelling would get Lorenzo Cicolla out of her system. She flirted with the thought for a while, then ruefully decided that running away from reality never solved problems, it only generated a few more, and made it to the theatre with only minutes to spare.

Her ticket was for one of the prime seats and the place was packed. The play had received rave reviews throughout its run and there didn't appear to be a single free seat. She found herself between a refined, grey-haired woman on her left and a prosperous, overweight businessman on her right.

There was only a cast of five in the play, which relied heavily on content and not at all on stage effects, and the acting was brilliant. She found herself wishing that she had seen more of Abigail's work, but the nearest theatre to where she lived was a tiny venue, manfully upkept, but really only patronised by the town's ardent dramatic society, several school plays, and pantomimes at Christmas.

And Abigail was a star way out of that league. She had a natural way of acting that enticed you into her make-believe world and held you there for the duration.

By the time the intermission came around, everyone was on edge, wondering what would happen in the second half.

Rather than beat a path to the theatre bar to get herself an orange juice, she stayed put, reading through the programme in front of her and smiling at the lavish praise quoted about her friend by the critics. Who would have thought it? she wondered. At ten, holding hands in the playground and giggling over all the things that occupied the minds of ten-year-old girls, who would ever have imagined that their lives would have turned out this way?

She snapped shut the programme. There was no point in going over her past relentlessly. She would never be able to dodge what had happened, but it was within her hands to mould the future.

She only wished that she could make her mind listen to this piece of wisdom instead of shoving images of Lorenzo down her throat all the time.

It was a relief when the bell sounded for the end of the interval and she could lose herself in the second half of the play.

By the time the play had wound its way to its conclusion, the audience had worked itself up to an emotional response. There was a standing ovation as the cast walked on to the stage and held hands, bowing to the appreciative crowd. Bouquets of flowers were brought on for Abigail, the only female lead in the play, and one of the actors said, with mock dismay, 'Where's mine?' which had everyone laughing.

She was preparing to pick her bag up when she heard Abigail's voice, ringing out as the applause died down.

'And now, I should like to break with tradition and do something absolutely unheard-of!'

There was a rustle of curiosity and then silence fell over the vast, packed hall. Nothing captured an audience more than the unexpected, and this was something totally unexpected. Isobel found that she was holding her breath. She suspected that quite a few in the audience were doing the same thing as well.

'I should like,' Abigail continued, 'with the kind permission of my fellow actors and yourselves, to ask my dearest friend Isobel to step down on to the stage here with me!'

Isobel's eyes widened in shock and she thought, Oh, God, but she had to walk down. She felt her legs teetering precariously as she moved past the rows of seats, all eyes fixed on her, and as she cleared the sea of onlookers Abigail smiled down at her and said, looking up, 'And, of course, I should also like to call Lorenzo Cicolla on to the stage as well.'

At which point Isobel felt as though everything happening was part of some wild, improbable dream. She didn't dare raise her eyes, but as she was ushered on to the stage through the side and took her place next to Abigail, she saw Lorenzo making his way up.

Abigail held her hand then, when Lorenzo was on stage, she announced, with disarming charm, 'To my two good friends, who have known me since childhood and who were always destined for each other. They have been through a few setbacks but they are here now, together, and together they must stay!'

There was tumultuous cheering. It rang from every quarter of the hall, rebounding on the walls and making Isobel feel light-headed.

She hardly knew when her fingers entwined with Lorenzo's. She looked up into that beloved, handsome, dark face and someone from the crowd roared out, 'Propose to the girl!'

'Lorenzo...' Isobel said, and there was a hush.

'Isobel.' His light eyes met hers and she felt her body trembling. 'Will you marry me?'

CHAPTER TEN

'WE HAVE to get out of here,' Lorenzo said. 'We have to talk.'

They were backstage, swirled off among the cast and the various assortment of people—in this case vastly outnumbering the members of the cast—who were heartily congratulating themselves on their performances.

Abigail walked over to them, her face flushed with success, and with a small, satisfied smile on her lips.

'I hope you didn't mind my impromptu behaviour,' she said, grinning and not looking too worried.

Isobel had moved away from Lorenzo. She still felt as though she was caught up in some elaborate dream, and was therefore finding it easy to disregard what had sounded like a proposal of marriage half an hour ago.

Dream or no dream, there was no way that he had meant a word of it anyway.

Standing in front of a crowd of hundreds, what else could he do? In fact, thinking about it, she rather blamed Abigail after all.

'You're an incorrigible romantic, Abby,' she said, not looking at Lorenzo, but very much aware of him standing next to her in his dark suit, impeccably handsome and very unnerving.

'I try my best,' Abigail replied, with a modest, thoughtful nod. 'I guess you two would like to have some time together?' she asked.

'Yes,' Lorenzo murmured, at the very same time that Isobel shook her head and murmured,

'No.'

'Well, what's it to be?' She looked at both of them with what Isobel considered a rather poor show of looking innocently bemused. 'Yes? No? Maybe? We'll mull it over and get back to you?'

The director sidled up behind her, beaming with triumph, and Isobel could see that her friend was itching to get away and do a post mortem on her performance with him, so she said wearily, 'All right,' still not looking at Lorenzo.

'I know a small restaurant quite near,' he said softly, so close to her that she bristled with awareness. 'Go away, Abigail,' he said with a slow smile, 'and in case I don't get around to telling you this, you're the most conniving female I've ever met in my life.' He was smiling though. Isobel could hear it in his voice.

He pulled her towards the exit and as soon as they were outside, with the cold air stinging her face, she turned to him and said, looking down, 'I know what marriage is for you. I know you didn't mean it.' Her voice sounded stiff and nervous, which she thought was a pretty good indication of how she was feeling.

'Oh, you *know*, do you?' he mocked, with just enough of a teasing drawl for her to risk a glance at him from under her lashes.

'Well, what else could you do? With the crowd after you for a . . . a . . .' She spluttered into silence.

'Later,' he said. 'This isn't the place for any kind of conversation. Come on.' He linked her arm through his and they walked in silence until they came to a small Italian restaurant, where the manager took one look at Lorenzo, smelled the power and wealth which he radiated, and ushered them to a discreet table in the corner of the room.

There was a small vase of carnations on the table and Lorenzo moved them.

'I want to see you when I say what I have to say, Isobel,' he murmured, which instantly made the coil in her stomach harden.

'I had no idea that she would pull a stunt like that,' Isobel mumbled. 'How did she know where to find you?'

'Savoy,' he said succinctly, staring at her intently until she felt her colour begin to rise. 'When I saw her on Broadway I took her out for a meal a couple of days later and I told her that the Savoy was the only place I stayed when I was in London. I never knew that the information would rebound on me.'

There was a warmth about him that was beginning to make her head spin, and it was a relief when the waiter came to take their order.

With typical Italian exuberance, everything they wanted was 'just beautiful' or 'a wonderful choice'.

'Was your mother all right about my hasty departure?' Lorenzo asked, and Isobel twiddled with the stem of her wine-glass.

'Yes.'

'And you? Were you all right?'

'Why on earth shouldn't I have been?'

'Because, my darling, we hardly parted on amicable terms.'

My darling. Had he called her 'my darling'? Without sarcasm?

'This is hopeless,' he said abruptly, standing up. The manager, in a flurry of alarm, flew over to their table and made a great fuss over this unexpected situation.

'There is something wrong?' he asked anxiously. 'You do not find my place agreeable?'

'Perfectly agreeable,' Lorenzo assured him, delving into his wallet and extracting a wad of notes. 'I'm sure the food would have been exquisite, but we find that we're in no mood to eat.' He looked at her through his lashes and Isobel mumbled confused agreement, getting to her feet and wondering what was going on.

They left the restaurant, took a taxi, and arrived at the Savoy in what seemed a breathlessly short space of time.

'Why are we here?' she asked in a high-pitched voice.

'To talk.' He shot her an innocent look. 'I can't talk to you in between mouthfuls of chicken cacciatore.'

He walked inside the hotel with Isobel following in his wake and, even though she knew where he was taking her, she still balked when they arrived at his bedroom and he unlocked the door and pushed it open.

'Why do we need to talk in a bedroom?' Her voice now resembled a squeak.

How could you do this to me, Abigail? she wailed to herself.

'Keep quiet,' he ordered, shutting the door behind them and tossing the keys on to the table in the middle of the room. 'Sit down. Have a drink and listen to what I've got to say.'

He poured them both a glass of whisky and soda, which was a drink she never indulged in, but which she now gratefully swallowed because her nerves were in serious danger of seizing up completely.

'Not your favourite drink, I know,' he said, sitting next to her.

'You remember,' she whispered.

'Of course I do. I remember,' he said on a sigh, 'everything about you, Isobel. How could I forget when you've been in my mind for so long?'

She didn't look at him. She hung her head and he brushed the curtain of black hair away so that he could see her profile. She felt the feathery touch of his fingers and shivered.

'Look at me,' he said, and she turned her head so that they were facing each other on the sofa. 'I spent four years with thoughts of you eating away inside me,' he continued, and there was nothing teasing in his light eyes. They were deadly serious, inward-thinking. 'I went to Chicago and every success, every pot of gold I found at the end of every rainbow, was marred by my bitter memories of you.'

'I did what I did——!' Isobel began, and he placed his finger over her lips.

'Shh.' He brushed her hair back from her face and his hand remained there, his fingers curled into her hair, as though he couldn't bring himself to take it away. 'You have no idea how much I loved you when you threw that bombshell at me,' he murmured, which pierced her heart.

All those years ago, of course she had known that he had loved her, but to hear him say it now made her want to sob.

'You were my sun, Isobel. I adored you. I always knew that you could have had anyone. The whole eligible male population of that damned town fancied themselves in love with you!' He grinned ruefully, and she could tell that he was thinking back. 'When you told me that you were going to marry Jeremy, I suspected that there was a reason, but I guess it was easy to believe when he announced that he was more suitable for you. And when you didn't deny it...'

'How could I?'

'I see that now, but I didn't then,' Lorenzo said in that deep, caressing voice that did strange things to her nervous system. 'All I saw were two people who shared the same background, and myself, a dangerous interloper, who had had the audacity to fall in love with the wrong girl. You have never been vain, Isobel, but what was said about you would have made your head spin.

You always had that incredible effect on the opposite sex, without even really seeming to realise it. It was almost as if you cast a spell wherever you walked. I could have killed him when he took you away from me—killed you both! Instead I went away.'

She didn't want to interrupt. Lorenzo was travelling down his own bitter lane of memories and she knew that he had to say it all.

She wanted to hear, too. She wanted to hear everything, with no bits missing, even though in her heart of hearts she knew where this confession was leading.

He had once loved her, he said. She had once been his sun, he said. But that was a long time ago. Now all that fierce, youthful energy had died. Wasn't that why he could speak to her so calmly? It was easy to speak with calm to someone when indifference was all that you felt for them.

'At that point I suppose I nurtured vague thoughts of returning one day, returning with all the money and power that Jeremy had said you needed.'

'So you did.'

'So I did,' he answered steadily, 'although circumstances were rather different from what I originally had in mind. But then life's like that, isn't it? One minute your route's stretching out in front of you, straight and clear, and the next minute it's dissolved into a network of paths and trails, and you haven't got a clue where the hell you're heading.'

He was still stroking her hair, and she wished that he wouldn't. It disorientated her. She wanted to be calm like him, to be able to tell him about her past in the same controlled voice, as though it was something to look back on with forgiveness, as though it no longer had the power to hurt.

'I was shocked when I heard about that car accident.'

'But you saw your chance to settle debts with me.'

'I knew that I had to return. I never once stopped to question it.'

They looked at each other. The room seemed terribly silent. He had switched on one of the table-lamps and there were a lot of half-shadows, pools of darkness.

'I thought,' he continued slowly, 'that I could bury the past once and for all, but when I saw you in that office all the old anger came rushing back. I looked at that exquisite, angelic face of yours and all I could see was you on your wedding-day. I wanted you then as I've never wanted anyone or anything in my whole life. I hadn't planned to force you into marriage, but when I looked at you I knew that I *had* to have you, that you *had* to be mine.'

'Hate is a powerful emotion, Lorenzo,' she mumbled, blinking back an embarrassing attack of tears.

'Hate?' He gave her an incredulous stare and her heart skipped a beat. 'I don't hate you, Isobel. Is that what you think?'

'Not now, perhaps.' She felt utterly miserable. 'Indifference now, perhaps.'

'How could I ever be indifferent to you?' He leaned forward and cupped her face in his hands. Strong, powerful hands that evoked a million memories for her.

Her heart was definitely doing wild things now. Soaring and swooping and flying high above the clouds. She held her breath and felt as if she was walking on the edge of a precipice.

'I'm in love with you, woman,' he said in an odd voice. 'I never stopped being in love with you. I wanted to. Dammit, I wanted to more than anything else in the world. I came back to put you into perspective but the only thing I succeeded in doing was falling even deeper in love with you all over again. But I couldn't block out the past. I had to know and, in between loving you, I wanted to damn well throttle you into telling me why you had married him.'

'Lorenzo!' She looked at him with shining eyes. 'You love me.'

She reached out tentatively and stroked his face and he groaned, bending to kiss her. His lips were hungry and searching and she clung to him, kissing him back.

'When I discovered the reason for your marriage, I saw red,' he muttered against her neck and she cradled his head in her hands. 'All I could think was: she didn't trust me enough. I came up here to London, but it's been a nightmare. At first I couldn't think straight, then I began to see the position you had found yourself in. I began to understand why you had acted the way you did. Oh, my darling...!' His voice was hoarse.

'I was imprisoned for four years,' Isobel said softly. 'All that time, the only things that kept me going were thoughts of you and my parents. I accepted marriage to Jeremy because I had no choice, but I didn't like it.'

'Didn't your parents guess?'

'I think they probably guessed,' Isobel said. 'They knew that there was something not quite right, but what could they do? Whenever they mentioned it, I backed away. I couldn't afford for either of them to suspect anything. I had done it for them, because I loved them so much, and I never regretted it. But how I regretted you. I built a future in my head, the future we should have had.'

'It must have made you terribly bitter towards him,' Lorenzo said gently, and she sighed.

'To start with. No, I suppose I was very bitter for the long course of my marriage to Jeremy, but the human being isn't capable of sustained anger. After a while, you begin to adapt the only way you can and I suppose, towards the end, I felt sorry for him, even though I knew that he had used me—used us both, in a way.'

'Poor darling Isobel.' He kissed her again, slowly and tenderly, pushing her back against the sofa. Her pulses began to quicken and she moaned as he stroked her waist through the fine material of her dress.

When he lifted her off the sofa and carried her towards the bedroom it was, she knew, the moment she had been waiting all those years for. The moment when he would touch her, without anger or unwanted desire, but with love.

He rested her on the bed, and she turned to him and said softy, 'I love you, Lorenzo Cicolla. I never stopped. Even when we argued bitterly, I still loved you. Nothing could kill that. Jeremy might have thought that by marrying me he had destroyed what we had, but he was wrong. He could never touch me, not deep inside where it counts.'

'He was unstable,' Lorenzo murmured, shrugging out of his shirt to expose his bronzed torso. He lay down beside her on his side and ran his hand along her, outlining the smooth contours of her body. 'Even before all that business happened, before he found out about his mother, there was something reckless about him. He was always like a keg of gunpowder waiting to explode.'

He unzipped her dress and she wriggled out of it, smiling slightly as he watched her, fascinated, as if he were seeing her for the first time.

When he touched her breast she lay back flat on the bed, her breathing coming and going quickly, as if she had run a marathon.

'You're so beautiful,' he murmured. 'The worst thing was that I understood why he wanted you so desperately. You provoke some dark, masculine instinct to be put under lock and key.'

'I hope not!' She laughed. Was she really *that* beautiful? She would have to look hard at herself the next time she found herself in front of a mirror.

'No, that would be a crime, wouldn't it?' He kissed her neck, then moved down her body, kissing every inch of her, exploring her with exquisite thoroughness.

She writhed as he caressed her stomach with his lips before nuzzling the soft mound of her femininity.

There was no anger, no resentment, no feeling of being in the unwilling grip of a passion too strong to control, much as you wanted to control it.

This was like the tenderness they had shared when they were younger, before life had begun to take its toll, except that this time there was a maturity about them that had been missing then.

She reached down and curled her fingers in his hair, parting her legs and opening her body to his eager exploration.

She sighed with contentment as he moved back up to lick her full breasts, taking each nipple into his mouth and teasing it until she wanted to scream.

When he finally came into her it was like being at home, where she belonged. Her body jerked against him, building to a crescendo, and her thought processes shut down as sensation took over.

'And now,' he said later, leaning on his elbow to look at her, 'that we're alone together, and there aren't hundreds of people watching, will you marry me, my darling Isobel? For all the right reasons?'

'Will I marry you?' She laughed and stroked his cheek. 'Yes. Yes, I will marry you. I've been waiting half my life for this moment, my love!'

And this time, she thought much later, as their love-making carried them through the night, who knew? There might even be a baby on the way.

EPILOGUE

ISOBEL looked at the suitcase in front of her. She would never have thought that she could look at Jeremy's possessions so calmly, so contentedly, without bitterness, but she could. Lorenzo had done that, she knew. Seven months ago they had married, a quiet affair involving only relatives and a few close friends. It had been the happiest day of her life and she had made sure that she had not worn white.

She smiled and began packing the last of the clothes, which she had only now got around to doing.

Where had the time gone? She knew, of course—redecorating their cottage together, making up for lost time.

She was about to close the suitcase when she felt something hard at the bottom of it, inside a zipped pocket. Curiously, she pulled out a notebook and began to read.

Her father's notebook, full of his usual jottings. It only took fifteen minutes and at the end of it she sat back on her heels and smiled. Somewhere, deep down, she had *known* that he would never have embezzled that money. Maybe it had crossed his mind, idle notes that had changed her life, but here, in this notebook, was the rest of the story. The bank loan, the figures carefully worked out, money which had never been stolen.

Jeremy had kept it all hidden. He had chosen to show her only enough to guarantee her co-operation.

Quietly she closed the suitcase, and stood it in the corner of the room. In the morning the last bits and pieces would be disposed of to a charity shop, in preparation for the young couple moving in over the weekend.

Then she went across to the window and looked out, still smiling, still holding that notebook.

Lorenzo would smile too when he read all this. He wouldn't fly off the handle. Marriage, he was fond of telling her in a semi-grumbling voice, had tamed the tiger, had domesticated him.

And, of course, something else too.

She patted her stomach contentedly and decided that *she* hadn't tamed him, not nearly as much as the tiny baby inside her.

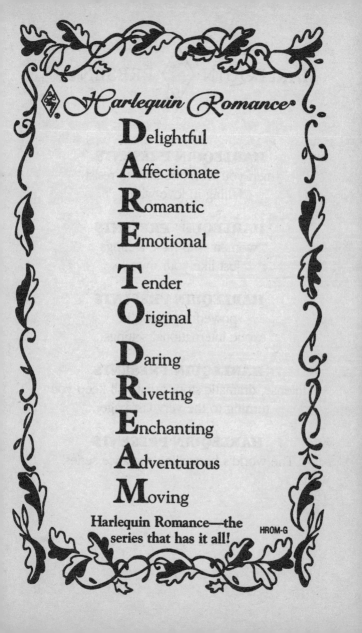

Harlequin Romance

Delightful

Affectionate

Romantic

Emotional

Tender

Original

Daring

Riveting

Enchanting

Adventurous

Moving

Harlequin Romance—the
series that has it all!

HROM-G

HARLEQUIN PRESENTS®

HARLEQUIN PRESENTS
men you won't be able to resist
falling in love with...

HARLEQUIN PRESENTS
women who have feelings
just like your own...

HARLEQUIN PRESENTS
powerful passion in
exotic international settings...

HARLEQUIN PRESENTS
intense, dramatic stories that will keep you
turning to the very last page...

HARLEQUIN PRESENTS
The world's bestselling romance series!

Harlequin® Historical

From rugged lawmen and
valiant knights to defiant heiresses
and spirited frontierswomen,
Harlequin Historicals will
capture your imagination with
their dramatic scope, passion
and adventure.

Harlequin Historicals…
they're too good to miss!

HHGENR